·SIMPLE GIFTS·

· SIMPLE GIFTS ·

The Story of the Shakers

JANE YOLEN

Illustrated by Betty Fraser

THE VIKING PRESS   NEW YORK

ACKNOWLEDGMENTS

My special thanks to the following people who helped me with my research: Dr. Frances Holmes, librarian of Mt. Toby Friends Meeting, in Leverett, Massachusetts; Mrs. Margaret Cantwell, librarian in Hatfield, Massachusetts; and Brother Ted Johnson, Director of the Shaker Museum at Sabbathday Lake in Maine. And a round of applause to Linda Zuckerman, editor and friend, who knows how to ask the right questions.

FIRST EDITION

Text Copyright © Jane Yolen, 1976
Illustrations Copyright © Viking Penguin Inc., 1976
All rights reserved
First published in 1976 by The Viking Press
625 Madison Avenue, New York, N.Y. 10022
Published simultaneously in Canada by
The Macmillan Company of Canada Limited

Printed in U.S.A.

1 2 3 4 5 80 79 78 77 76
Library of Congress Cataloging in Publication Data
Yolen, Jane H   Simple gifts: the story of the shakers
Bibliography: p.   Includes index.
Summary: Traces the rise and decline of the Shakers
who immigrated to the United States from England
in 1774, settling throughout New England.
1. Shakers—Juvenile literature. [1. Shakers]
I. Fraser, Betty. II. Title. BX9771.Y67 289.8 76–14420
ISBN 0–670–64584–2

For MARILYN E. MARLOW,
who tries to keep me
from getting too complex

Author's Note

I BEGAN this book with a respect for the Shakers, for their famous handwork and their communal way of life. Partway through the research I changed my mind. The Shakers, I thought, were American eccentrics in the extreme, perhaps even individually—and as a group—certifiably insane. Their ideas of the dual sexual nature of God, their absolute adherence to laws of celibacy, and their marching worship meetings made me uncomfortable. I wanted, in my discomfort, to laugh.

But by the time I had finished writing the book and had visited one of the two remaining Shaker communities—Sabbathday Lake—I had changed my mind again. Today I am filled with the spirit of this peculiar people. *Peculiar* is not my word; it is the word that one of the Sabbathday Lake sisters, Sister Mildred Barker, uses to describe the Shakers. Their spirit is a blending of joy and peace and hard work. Though their movement is moribund, it is not yet dead. It is still changing and evolving, a living organism.

The question remains: Is Shakerism an anachronism, an idea and spirit out of its proper time? Indeed, does it have a proper time? I do not know.

But this I do know: The ghosts of the old Shakers spoke to me quite strongly while I was at Sabbathday Lake. And their message, even when their strange methods are rejected, can speak to anyone today. This is the message: God is within anyone who accepts Him. Put your hands to work and your hearts to God. All things are possible in this world, even the making of heaven on earth. And this last, the Shakers believe, they have already done.

—*Jane Yolen*

PHOENIX FARM
HATFIELD, MASSACHUSETTS

Contents

O THE SIMPLE GIFTS OF GOD

O the simple gifts of God,
They're flowing like an ocean,
And I will strive with all my might
To gather in my portion.

I love, I love the gifts of God,
I love to be partaker,
And I will labor day and night
To be an honest Shaker.

—NORTH UNION,
OHIO SQUARE ORDER SHUFFLE SONG

SIMPLE GIFTS

'Tis the gift to be simple, 'tis the gift to be free,
'Tis the gift to come down where we ought to be,
And when we find ourselves in the place just right,
'Twill be in the valley of love and delight.

When true simplicity is gain'd,
To bow and to bend we shan't be ashamed,
To turn, turn will be our delight
Till by turning, turning we come round right.

—ALFRED MINISTRY, JUNE 28, 1848

One foot up, the other down,
Tread the serpent to the ground.
—SONG FROM SABBATHDAY LAKE

The Shaker Phenomenon

April 1784

1 THE house is like other New England houses, plain
and sturdy. It is large, well built, with fireplaces in
each of the rooms, for the owner is a man of means. But
the house differs from the other houses in the village because it is no longer just a house. It has become a place
where people come to worship.

The worship service is beginning. Inside about twenty
men and women sit silently in the parlor, men on one side
of the room, women on the other.

Almost all the women are dressed in long gray or blue
dresses with white kerchiefs across their shoulders. They
seem especially quiet. The men, wearing wide-brimmed
hats and dressed in breeches and coats, give the ap-
pearance of quiet barely contained.

Suddenly one of the women throws her head back, her face flushed and shining. She is small, scarcely larger than a child, but her voice fills the room with song. There are no discernible words to her song. She sings a lilting "la, la, la" that flows freely and formlessly. The women on both sides of her pick up the free song and add their voices to it. They follow her lead, always half a note or so behind her. A few of the men join in, humming low, throaty notes.

All at once, the first woman leaps up and throws her arms in the air. Her song takes on words. "Love, love, love," she sings.

The other women jump up raggedly, singing with her. "Love, love, love."

A plump woman, about middle age, in dark gingham, starts turning slowly in place, her hands held high above her.

"Love, Mother's love," she croons.

"Mother's love, Mother's love," sing the men back, and one of them, a black-haired giant of a man, shouts out, "I leap, I fly." He leaps into the air. His fingers scrape the ceiling.

And then it is pandemonium. Everyone begins to jump and spring into the air, some taking small rabbit hops up and down in place, others leaping as if to gain the sky.

And all the while, the plump gingham-clad woman turns round, faster and faster, singing to herself, "Love, Mother's love."

The first woman, the small one, stops jumping and

begins to shake. Her tremblings become violent; another woman puts her arms around her and they stand together, trembling and shaking and crying in soft singing voices, "Joy, joy, joy," over and over and over again.

It is now an hour later. Hot and exhausted, the men have removed their coats and hats. The women mop their foreheads with their handkerchiefs.

The parlor is almost quiet once more. The women hug and bless one another. The men do the same. At no time in all the shaking and trembling and dancing and singing has a man touched a woman or a woman touched a man.

They return to their seats for a few moments of silence, and then depart.

Fifty years later the Shakers were still meeting but things were very different. In the first place, the meeting site was changed. They gathered instead in one of several barrel- or gambrel-roofed meeting houses in New England. The meeting houses, painted a stark white, were unadorned and had neither carved entrances nor shutters. The Shakers considered such things frivolous and worldly.

The men and women dressed in a kind of uniform. The men wore blue and white pantaloons, blue coats, and black waistcoats. The women dressed in long white gowns, blue petticoats, and blue and white aprons. White muslin caps hid their faces so well, a visitor once remarked of the Shaker sisters, that "a stranger is at first unable to distinguish the old from the young."

That visitor was only one of many who came to watch

the strange Shaker ceremonies in the vast meeting houses. They sat on benches and snickered and stared while two or three hundred Shakers performed intricate dance sequences with such names as the Square Order Shuffle, the Hollow Square, the Endless Chain or the Wheel Dance. The singing and dancing were now so well ordered and regimented that any army officer who visited claimed it was exactly like an army field day since "there was such a scene of marching and counter marching, slow step, quick step, and double-quick step, advancing and retiring, forming open column and close column, perpendicular lines and oblique lines, that it was sufficient to puzzle and confound the clearest head of the lookers-on."

Only occasionally would the orderliness break down and frenetic scenes from earlier, emotional meetings repeat themselves. Then once more men would leap to the ceilings and land so hard they jarred the meeting room. Women would spin in place, tremble, or fall down with great gasps of hysterical laughter. Then the meetings were called "quick meetings" or known as a "Shaker high."

One of the most prominent of the visitors was the journalist Horace Greeley, who went to a meeting in 1838. He was present during a quick meeting and wrote: "What was a measured dance became a wild, discordant frenzy; apparent design or regulation is lost; and grave manhood and gentler girlhood are whirling round and round, two or three in company, and then each for him or herself." Greeley's account was read and reread by many Americans, along with those of other reporters, who likened the Shakers to "penguins in procession," "dancing dogs" or kangaross. Greely convinced the public that the Shakers were pure American eccentrics locked up in asylums of their own creation. And for years most people knew only this about the Shakers—that they sang and danced with an hysterical frenzy that led to trembling, quaking, and falling down in fits.

There are barely a handful of true Shakers left today. They live in two communities that are little more than museums: Sabbathday Lake in Maine and Canterbury in New Hampshire. Yet the Shakers have left a truly American legacy, a legacy of hard work and strong belief, of courage under pressure, and a philosophy that is a strange blending of order and passion.

But if that were all they left, why did the Shakers endure for so long? Why were they—are they—the longest-lived utopian or idealistic and visionary group in America? How did they come together and what were they seeking? Where are they going and why are there almost no more of them?

The final answer to all those questions is simply this: The Shakers were a phenomenon, a special kind of group and group experience. They are themselves both the question and the answer, a question and an answer that began in England two hundred years ago when an illiterate thirty-six-year-old factory worker, Ann Lee, woke up in prison one morning convinced she was God.

Mother Ann and the Blessed Fire: 1736–1772

2 ANN LEE was a short, pleasant-faced Englishwoman. There was little about her that suggested the prophet, even less that suggested the divine. She could not read or write; she was trained for no profession; she had no special skills. Yet when she came out of prison in 1772 claiming to be the Second Coming incarnate, the female counterpart of Jesus, the issuer-in of the Millennium, she was believed. She was believed by a hardy—some would say foolhardy—band of followers.

This strange and unique woman was born on Toad Lane in Manchester, England, in 1736. The world she was born into was a world where babies died every day in squalid, filthy rooms, never having seen the sunlight. She was lucky to be alive. No one remarked her birth except her mother and father. Newborns in the poorer houses of England were rarely recorded. Later, Shaker tradition would place her birth on February 29, a magical date.

Her father John Lee (or as it was sometimes spelled on documents Lees) made a meager living as a blacksmith which he supplemented by tailoring. In Manchester, few people but the owners enjoyed the prosperity that the new textile mills had brought. Most of the common folk worked hard from early morning through a long day, and spent what little money they earned on food and the numbing drink served up in the grog shops. It has been said of Manchester at that time that there were more grog shops than churches, and of churches there were a goodly number.

Even working two jobs was not enough. John Lee could barely feed and clothe his eight children. He certainly could not afford to send them to school. So they grew up as illiterate as he, as illiterate as their friends and neighbors. Indeed, it was the rare individual in the eighteenth century English slums who could read or write.

From the beginning, Ann Lee was different from her brothers and sisters. Though she was far from ethereal looking, being a chunky, brown-haired child and later a short, stocky woman, she believed herself to be a divine spirit. Like another illiterate dreamer, the fifteenth century Jeanne d'Arc, she had heavenly visions when she was young. But where Joan of Arc saw herself as God's strong right hand in the liberation of France, Ann Lee's visions were more grandiose. She saw herself as God's own child "conjured from the loins of the firmament." Indeed, young Ann, by her own accounting, would often stare into a mirror trying to catch sight of the wings she expected to sprout from her shoulders at any minute.

Still, as divine as she imagined herself to be, Ann had to help add to the family's small income. And so, as soon as she was old enough to work the long hours expected of her, she was sent out to the textile mills. At thirteen she was a cutter of velvet, progressing from there to shearing hat fur and preparing cotton for the looms. By the time she was twenty, like many girls her age she had worked for nearly half her life at low-paying, brutal jobs that did nothing to lift the young workers spiritually, mentally, or physically. It was dull, grinding, life-destroying work. And Ann hated it.

She left finally to become a cook in a public infirmary, a "house with twelve beds." It was there, amid the sick of body, the sick of mind, and the dying, that Ann Lee was first able to reach out and help others.

But it was not enough. The visionary child had grown into a grave and solemn woman. She saw firsthand how poverty, illiteracy, the spiraling birthrate, and mind-destroying, grueling work ate into the souls of the men and women. She saw how these things drove people to drink and to violence, and made them susceptible to disease and early death. Her piercing blue eyes, eyes which would later be described as "penetrating" and "filled with power," saw visions of an alternate world, an infinitely better world. Yet she did not know how to find the path to that world.

Then in 1758 she met Jane and James Wardley and

through them met men and women who were visionaries and seekers like herself.

The Wardleys had begun as Quakers, a religious group established one hundred years earlier. They believed in the use of silence in their worship, were against wars and personal violence, and preached that God did not live far off in heaven but dwelt inside every man, woman, and child. The early Quakers had been among the most militant of the dissenting religious groups in England, breaking into church meetings and railing against both priest and "steeple house," as they called the church. But eighteenth century Quakerism was much quieter. Certainly it was too tame and serious for the Wardleys.

Like many others of the lower and middle classes of eighteenth century England, the Wardleys looked to religion for their entertainment as well as for their salvation. Ever since the Bible had been translated into English and widely distributed around the country, every man and woman who could read—even those who couldn't—considered themselves experts on dogma. In a sense, arguing theology was the national sport in England and had been for two hundred years. The Wardleys, remembering the early passion of the Quakers, joined the sect.

However, Quakerism paled quickly for the Wardleys. They wanted something more exciting, something with ceremony as well as silence. They looked further, and what they found were the Camisards.

The Camisards were a mystical Protestant group that

worshiped in trances and fasts and shaking fits. In France they had been known as the Prophets and, more sarcastically, "Les Trembleurs," the Shakers. Driven out of France, they had arrived in London in 1706 and had just about died out when the Wardleys discovered them. They were just what James and Jane Wardley had been looking for. Yoking the Camisard's trembling hysteria with the Quaker's idea of the God within, the Wardleys began their own sect. They invited like-minded friends to meetings at their home where they held secret worship services far into the night.

The meetings were not strictly legal, and to outsiders they might have seemed heretical and devil-oriented because of their strange, exotic ceremonies. Heresy was a punishable crime.

The worshipers would begin by sitting silently, Quaker style, for many minutes. Then suddenly one or another of those attending would begin to tremble or cry out, scream, sob, or shake. And then the "shaking" part of the meeting would begin in earnest. Soon the worshipers were given the name "Shaking Quakers." Their meetings were not as secret as they had supposed.

The Wardleys' home meetings appealed to the twenty-two-year-old Ann Lee for many reasons. First, most of the people were of the same background as she and she felt comfortable among them. The Wardleys were tailors, the others simple laborers, millworkers, and the like. They were people who had worked since childhood and who believed that life had to have a spiritual meaning as well as a worldly one. Most important, these were people who, like Ann Lee, were visionaries. Often in the meetings they would go into trances, see strange lights in the sky, or hear heavenly voices.

Such mystical experiences were not limited to the Shakers. Every religion, every sect both large and small, has had members who have gone into trances. Ezekiel saw a wheel in the air, Moses a burning bush, the Virgin Mary appeared to children at Lourdes. There are religions whose members train methodically to develop their mystical states of mind with fasting and concentration and body control, such as the Yogis of India. There are religions such as the peyote-eating Indians of America's Southwest, whose members create their trances with hallucinogens. And there are nonreligious people who go into trances in very nonreligious places: World War II soldiers in far-apart foxholes saw rainbows in the sky and felt a great sense of peace; teenagers in rock concerts have passed out in ecstacy; prisoners in solitary confinement have had insights into their conditions. They all see things that are not of the "real" world. What they have in common is this: The person in the trance has the absolute conviction of the truth of that trance. He or she *has been there.* There is no arguing it.

So it was with the first Shakers at the Wardleys' house. They shared no rigid doctrines, no laws, or rules. What they shared was a belief in three things: the absolute truth of their visions; the fact that the Millennium or Second Coming of Christ and the reign of peace was at hand; and the radical insistence that God was returning to Earth as a woman.

For nine years Ann Lee worshiped with the Wardleys. She was very close to them, calling them Mother Jane and Father James. The Wardleys demanded total devotion to themselves and their cause. Ann Lee was willing to give it. At this point they were the leaders, strong and unbending; Ann Lee was a follower. During those nine years, Ann Lee's personal life was undergoing a number of changes.

In January 1762 Ann Lee was pressured into marrying her father's apprentice, Abraham Stanley (or, as some records show, Standerin). It was a bad match from the start. Stanley was a lusty, good-humored man who believed in the ability of his own hands and the heartiness of his own appetites. Ann Lee, on the other hand, was a mild-mannered but intense mystic who believed she could converse with God. The only thing they had in common was that neither could read.

Four times in four years Ann Lee Stanley became pregnant. Each time the child died at birth or soon after. Though such infant deaths were not unsual for families in all classes in the eighteenth century, it seemed to Ann a judgment—a judgment on her marriage, on all marriages, on the very institution of marriage.

When her last child, a girl named Elizabeth, died in 1766, Ann saw her own carnal life buried with the child.

Night after night following the infant's death Ann walked the floor in her stocking feet praying and weeping. She feared to fall asleep lest she "awake in hell." She avoided her husband's bed "as if it had been made of embers."

She saw the way to heaven to be the denial of "every gratification of a carnal nature." Weakened as she was by the recent birth, and emotionally drained by the deaths, Ann Lee decided that "carnal" nature meant not only sexual relations with her husband but also eating and drinking as well.

But abstaining from food and drink made her ill, and she eventually had to be fed by others. Yet a strange thing happened. As Ann Lee became weaker in body, she became stronger in spirit or, as she herself put it, her "soul broke forth to God." She described her conversion, her vision, in terms of childbirth, saying, "I felt as sensibly as ever a woman did a child, when she was delivered of it."

The struggle inside her was costly. She told later followers that as she paced the floors "bloody sweat" came through her pores and tears flowed down her cheeks until the skin "cleaved" off. She said she wrung her hands until blood "gushed from under [her] nails." The agitation, the sorrow, the wrestling with her problems was so intense that she groaned and cried out and once trembled so much her bed rocked violently. Poor Abraham, who was in it at the time, was "glad to leave it."

What Ann Lee was suffering was a kind of nervous breakdown brought on by the births and deaths of four children close together. Stillborn children and children dying in infancy were so common in the eighteenth century that many mothers at all levels of society suffered such breakdowns as a result. Some, like Queen Anne of England, who lost ten out of fifteen children to miscarriages and the rest but one in infancy, turned to hard and continual work to ward off depression. Some, like Polly—the wife of John Marshall, chief justice of the United States Supreme Court—who lost two children and went insane because of it, were kept locked up.

Ann Lee turned to God.

Would things have turned out differently if young Elizabeth Stanley had lived? Would Ann Lee have become a quiet, passive mother raising her girl as she, herself, had been raised, in the back alleyways of Manchester? There is no way of knowing. For the child was buried, and so was Ann Lee's married life. She turned entirely from her husband to the Wardleys and their followers. For it was the Shaking Quakers who had stood by her during her bereavements, not Stanley. They, not he, had helped her in her times of seeking. They, not he, had comforted and fed her in her time of trials.

The Ann who returned from the graveside of that last child was not the mild, passive Ann whom the Wardleys had known before. The new Ann Lee was a zealot. She was so filled with her new mission—her rage against the marriage bed—she soon converted them all.

The first and cardinal sin, Ann Lee informed them, was

"cohabitation of the sexes." Once it was gone, humankind would have a hope of salvation.

So the Shaking Quakers, who before had met without creed or rules, now had one. And it was a very definite *thou shalt not.*

Ann Lee's ideas were not based strictly on Scripture, nor were they *only* the result of the loss of her four babies. Her marriage had been, from the beginning, a loveless one. She and Abraham had fought so bitterly, in fact, that he had already complained of her to the cathedral authorities. And she had long been preaching against the sensual side of marriage, even angering her own father and brothers with her outbursts. It is surprising, therefore, that later she would number among her followers one of her brothers and her father, John Lee.

Up to this time, Ann had preached. Now she began to lay down the law. The Wardleys and their companions were amazed at the change in her. They attributed it, as did Ann herself, to the will of God. When she was arrested and imprisoned in 1772 for disturbing the Sabbath, none of her companions was surprised.

It was while in prison that she had her most important vision. When she emerged she was hailed by them all as "The Mother in Christ."

Oh I love Mother
I love her Power,
I know 'twill help me
In ev'ry trying hour. . . .
  —SONG FROM NEW LEBANON, 1847

Mother Ann's Power
1772–1774

3 THIS was not the first time Ann Lee had been arrested. The constable in Manchester had quite an account of her activities in 1772:

> *"To the Jurors Bailiff on prosecuting*
> *John Lees and his Daughter Ann. . . . 1*
> *shilling 6 pence"*

> *"To repairs making good the breaches at*
> *Lees in Toad Lane in order to apprehend*
> *a gang of Shakers locked up there . . . 5*
> *shillings 2 pence"*

There were others.

The Shakers, as they were now called, had been taking a hand in their own prophecies. They were no longer content with sitting in quiet parlors and suddenly bursting out in ecstatic singing and dancing. Now they were beginning

· 17 ·

to break into the regular church services as well. And each time they broke in, shouting out their heretical visions, they were arrested and thrown in jail. Ann Lee was involved in most of the disturbances.

Strange tales were circulating about the Shakers. Folk said they were witches, devil-worshipers engaged in fantastic revelries. The whisperings about them turned to mutterings, the mutterings to shouts. Soon mobs gathered, first to throw insults and next to throw stones.

Once such mob set out to stone Ann and four companions as they spoke. The five stood still and, according to Shaker texts, said not a word but gazed in love at their persecutors. Stones fell to the right of them and to the left, in front of them and behind. But not one of the Shakers was touched. Seeing this, the mob fled in panic.

Another time, according to Shaker histories, one of Ann's own brothers became enraged as she sat in a chair singing loudly to herself about God. He took up a staff as large as a broom handle and stalked toward her.

"Ann," he called.

She did not respond.

"Will you not answer me?"

Filled with her own bright notions of God, she kept singing.

He was so angry then, the Shakers say, he began to beat her with the staff on the face, on the nose. The stick was soon in splinters, yet still she sang.

Her brother went into the kitchen to get himself a mug

of ale. Drinking it down quickly, he returned. She was still singing and smiling. He could not stand the insistent sound. Flinging the shattered stick aside, he beat her with his fists until he could hardly stand. Shaker journals note that Ann remained unmarked throughout the incident, and she never missed a note of her song.

The personal violence against Ann Lee and her Shaker friends kept on until at last even the authorities had to act. But instead of arresting the mobs, they arrested the few Shakers. Ann was accused of blasphemy, of mocking God. The four "learned ministers" who questioned her threatened to brand her cheek and stick a hot iron poker through her tongue for her misdeeds. It was not an unusual punishment in the eighteenth century. But Ann Lee stood up to the ministers and began to lecture them. She did not speak in English, however, but in a gibberish that Shakers called "tongues." Some Shakers claimed that she spoke that day in twelve separate languages, including French, Hebrew, Latin, and Greek. Others swore that she clearly articulated seventy-two different speeches. Whatever the truth, she was neither maimed nor branded. The judges were clearly frightened by her ability to speak in tongues, since they knew she was unschooled.

The judges may have been afraid, but the mob waiting outside the courtroom was not. They again tried to stone her, and when Ann walked through them unscathed, the angry townsfolk turned upon themselves. Many went home that day with broken limbs.

Ann Lee did not come out unscathed from her final English imprisonment. In the damp, dark stone jail her health was broken even as her spirit was uplifted.

She was arrested for the crime of interrupting the services at Manchester Cathedral in the summer of 1773. Found guilty, she was fined 20 pounds. It was an incredible sum. Today it would be equivalent to $1000. For someone as poor as Ann, who knew few ways of earning a living, the sum was an impossible one to raise. And so Ann Lee was sent to jail. For two weeks she was left in a dark stone cell, then sent on to the house of correction.

According to Ann Lee's own testimony, the first fourteen days were days of inhuman cruelty. The jailers, she claimed, locked her in a cell so small she could not fully straighten up. They brought her neither food nor drink. Surely they expected her to die, thus ridding Lancashire of one noisy, meddlesome, religious fanatic.

However, the Shaker journals say, the jailers did not reckon with the ingenuity and loyalty of Ann Lee's friends. One, the young, devoted James Whittaker, crept to the jail each night and poured wine through the keyhole of her cell. Thus he kept Ann Lee alive.

It is, however, a strange tale in several ways. According to full accounts of eighteenth-century English jails, prisoners were not regularly starved as part of their punishment, though they were given small rations. Second, Ann Lee was not a major offender—a murderer or a traitor who might have been beaten or even tortured as part of the regular regimen. She had been imprisoned for a minor infraction of the law—breaking the Sabbath. Third, the prisoners were not kept on either a basement or ground-level floor, according to scholars, but rather on a second floor. That naturally would have made it impossible for a friend to creep by and help.

Thus, the story is false.

Though the story does not hold together, it became one of the miracle stories widely believed by the Shakers. Such stories of sufferings and martyrdoms often seem an integral part of religious, social, or political movements. If a person is willing to defend a belief or principle, sacrificing even his or her life, it lends extra meaning to those beliefs or principles. The early stories about Mother Ann and the founders of Shakerism are full of details of beatings, hardships, and sufferings gladly entered into. In many religions there are similar instances of martyrdom.

In later years, when James Whittaker assumed a major role in the growing Shaker society, the story of how he kept Mother Ann alive while she lay in jail became one of the most famous incidents in early Shaker history.

Whether or not Ann Lee was miraculously sustained in the jail, the experience was injurious to her health. The cold and damp seeped into her bones and greatly contributed to her early death.

At the same time it contributed to her life—her spiritual life. It was here, in the Manchester jail, that Ann Lee had a vision. She saw played out before her the scene in Eden where, in her version, Adam and Eve committed the sexual act, which forever separated them from God.

No sooner had that vision ended than Ann Lee felt that the spirit of God had physically entered her. As she later told her friends, "Christ dwells within me."

In some ways this was not an unusual idea. Indeed, it was common for the English Quakers to say such things. It was their central belief that God dwelt within each individual. When Ann Lee said it, she meant something more.

She meant that the spirit of God was specifically part of her, Ann Lee, that she *was* God, was His special instrument. Ann Lee believed fully and firmly that she was the anointed successor to Jesus, that God was of a dual nature, both male and female, and had already appeared as male in Jesus. This time, the Second Coming, He was appearing in Ann Lee.

She left the dark prison by the Irwell River filled with religious hope and announced that she was "Ann the Word" and the "Bride of the Lamb."

She was so burning with this idea that she soon convinced the Wardleys and their followers.

Jane Wardley had been waiting for a number of years for such a revelation. It had already been her conviction, since joining the Camisards, that God would manifest Himself this time in a woman. So immediately she called Ann Lee "The candle of the Lord" and graciously accepted as her own title "John the Baptist in the female line." The Shaker succession was thus completed easily and seemingly without animosity.

A few days after leaving prison, in the house of John Townlet, Ann Lee was formally acknowledged as the new leader of the Shakers, supplanting the Wardleys. From then on, she was known as Mother Ann, "Mother of the new creation."

Mother Ann was swift in proclaiming that the day of judgment was at hand. She swore that the only salvation would be in total confession of sins and the swearing off of all fleshly practices. It was a simple enough doctrine. And, except for the force of Mother Ann's new magnetic personality, it was all the Shakers had to offer the world.

For ten months after Mother Ann had emerged from the womb of the prison, the Shakers lived and worshiped without further arrests or abuses. Their singing and dancing and trembling fits, their ecstatic visions and crying out in tongues were once more confined to small meetings in the houses of Shaker believers. But in this time their numbers did not grow. The same names, the same faces were seen and heard at each meeting: the Wardleys, the Lees, James Whittaker and a few others were constant. No one else joined.

Perhaps that is why the Shakers decided to go to a new country. However, the Shakers do not give that as the reason: They cite a series of revelations. Ann Lee saw again and again in visions that there was a chosen people waiting for her in America, specifically in New England. Finally, young James Whittaker had a similar dream.

It happened one night when the little band of Shakers was on its twenty-mile walk between meeting places. While they rested beside the road, Whittaker suddenly had a vision of a large tree whose "leaves shone with such brightness, as made it appear like a burning torch." That, he interpreted, was the church in America.

The Shakers decided to hold a special meeting to discuss going to America. And suddenly, every one of them had a confirming dream or vision.

America called. The Shakers listened. And then, as they wrote of it, they made the decision to go to America and "danced till morning."

They made their move in the spring of 1774. John Hocknell, the richest member of the band of Believers, booked passage for nine of them aboard the ship *Mariah*. The nine included Mother Ann's husband Abraham Stanley. He was not one of the Shakers, but he knew he had no future in England. If Hocknell was willing to pay for his passage to the New World, Stanley was willing to go. The others traveling on the *Mariah* were Mother Ann, her brother William Lee, the young James Whittaker, prosperous John Hocknell and his son Richard, James Shepherd, Mary Partington, and Nancy Lees. Two people were surprisingly missing: Jane and James Wardley. They had left the society of Believers a short time after Mother Ann had taken over. Evidently they had not really accepted Mother Ann as the leader of *their* worshipers. Thereafter the Wardleys disappeared from Shaker history.

The passage across the Atlantic was not easy. It was an arduous three-month voyage. The group of Believers insisted on worshiping up on deck, singing and dancing in their strange ecstatic way. It frightened the crew and so annoyed the captain that he threatened to have them all thrown overboard if they did not stop.

The Atlantic in spring is unpredictable. A sudden storm of surprising strength blew up and battered the small ship. A plank was pushed aside by the brutal waves. The *Mariah* began to ship water. Both passengers and crew took turns at the pumps, but it was no use. It was obvious to all that the ship was sinking.

Captain and crew prepared to abandon ship when Mother Ann pushed her way to them.

"Be of good cheer," she announced to the startled seamen. "For I was just now sitting by the mast and I saw a bright angel of God . . ."

At that very moment, an enormous wave slammed against the ship and knocked the loose hull planking back into place. The water stopped flowing in. The ship was saved.

That evening the crew joined the Shakers in their songs and dances of praise and the *Mariah* sailed on to America.

They landed in New York on August 6, 1774.

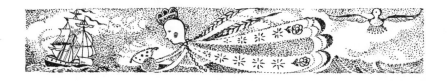

To mark their shining passage,
Good angels flew before,
Towards the land of promise,
Columbia's happy shore.

—FROM "MOTHER," SONG IN
MILLENNIAL PRAISES, PART II

Columbia's Happy Shore:
1774–1780

4 NEW YORK in 1774 was two towns joined by a dirt road. It contained less than 10,000 citizens. Eighteen languages were spoken and there were small pockets of the eighteen cultures from which each language sprang. Dutch lived with Dutch, French with French, English with English. There was already a newspaper, published first in 1725, and a university, founded in 1754. But for all that, New York was a small, dirty, brawling island port town with cows grazing in the small commons. It was not nearly as sophisticated or as proper as the English towns and cities that the small band of Shakers had known.

But it was a new land with a new people waiting. It was here, the Shakers believed, that the tree with the shining leaves would be planted and would grow.

Would they recognize the people who were to be their

followers? To Mother Ann, at least, there was no doubt. "I saw some of them in a vision," she told her disciples, "and when I meet them, I will know them."

And so they landed in New York City on a hot August day. It was not a good time for English men and women to come to America. Talk of rebellion, of revolution, was in the air. Enemies lists were being drawn up on both sides of the Atlantic. Choosing sides was a preoccupation in the colonies. But if the Shakers were even aware of the talk, they gave no sign. Their work was God's work, and as part of their Quaker legacy, they were opposed to violence in all its forms, and especially to war.

They came off the boat with neither friends nor relatives to aid them and wandered up "Broad Way." Coming on to Queen Street, Mother Ann was in the lead. She stopped suddenly in front of a house where a woman sat sunning herself.

Mrs. Cunningham, the mistress of the house, looked up at the people grouped in front of her. The three women were in traditional Quaker gray dresses, white handkerchiefs "pinned modestly across the top." The deep bonnets capping their heads cast no shadow across their faces and their eyes burned with fervor. The six men seemed a calmer lot, dressed more like English tradesmen, with broad-brimmed hats, long-tailed coats, and breeches buckled at the knees.

Mother Ann spoke. "I am commissioned to preach the everlasting gospel to America," she announced to the surprised Mrs. Cunningham. "An Angel commanded me to come to this house, and to make a home for me and my people."

According to Shaker journals, Mrs. Cunningham's surprise did not last long, for she took the travelers in and fed them. Though there was not room for all the Shakers, Mrs. Cunningham offered room and board to Mother Ann and her husband. In exchange, Ann was to work as a laundress in the house and Stanley would help in Mr. Cunningham's blacksmith shop.

The rest of the Shakers moved on to wait, as was their custom, for inspiration. Soon visions of a permanent home sent Hocknell, William Lee, and young Whittaker off into the wilderness of northern New York. There, with money from Hocknell's almost exhausted resources, they leased wood and swampland from a Dutch landholder. Working quickly, they built a crude log cabin and roughed out a farm so that in the spring they could bring the others up from New York City to their Niskayuna home.

In the spring, while the others set to work clearing and building for eternity, John Hocknell returned to England to fetch his wife. He had a legal battle on his hands, for his family had had him declared insane when he joined the Shakers. Hocknell wanted to bring over his wife, the rest of his money, and his good friend John Partington as well.

This is how matters stood with the small band of Believers. Scattered, poor, no help in sight, two existed in a city house, six in a swampy clearing, and one traveled back to a country and a family that considered him insane.

It was not a glorious beginning.

Mother Ann and her husband did not stay in the Cunningham house for long. Weakened by the trip and the weather, Abraham Stanley took sick in 1775. Mother Ann left her own work to nurse him.

The Cunninghams could not afford to support the two, and so put them out of the house. Without room and board, with no money, the two nearly starved. But the blacksmith at last recovered. And when he did, he gave up pleading with Mother Ann to resume marital relations with him and ran off with a woman of the streets. So Abraham Stanley exited ignobly from Shaker history.

On the eve of realizing her dream, Mother Ann was at the lowest point in her life. In a strange land, deserted by her husband, apart from her disciples, with no means to earn bread or bed, what was she to do? Her shelter consisted of an unheated, bedless room "with only a cold stove for a seat" and her food "a cruise of vinegar."

At that moment, a kind of miracle occurred. Hocknell returned from England accompanied by his wife. They found Mother Ann at Christmas time, having traced her from the Cunningham house. They fed her and took her up the Hudson to the clearing at Niskayuna, eight miles from Albany. There the other Shakers were hard at work building what would become their first communal home.

Life at Niskayuna was not easy. The Shaker brothers and sisters lived together in the crude log cabin that Hocknell, Lee, and Whittaker had roughed out. The women were on the first floor, the men on the second. When they were not clearing and building, or putting in the crops, the Shakers were hard at work cleaning, praying, and counseling the few hardy folk who found their way to the door.

Whenever possible converts entered their house, the Shakers gave up their own beds to the newcomers and slept on the cold floors. But they did not seek out the newcomers. The Shakers were simply too busy trying to make a place for themselves in the new land. And in three and a half years they could count only one new Shaker, their neighbor Eleanor Vedder.

Some of the Shakers worried about this. Again and again they asked Mother Ann when they could begin the work of spreading the word, planting that tree with the shining leaves. But Mother Ann was not only mystical. She was practical as well. She knew that first they had to have a place of their own. So she advised her companions to be patient.

"The time is near at hand when they will come like doves," she said.

Tho many foes beset me round
My self and pride and all that
Yet since the way of life I've found
I'll bear my cross for all that.
— SONG FROM NEW LEBANON, 1830

The American Venture: 1780—1784

5 THE Shakers waited three and a half years. The Declaration of Independence was signed and battles raged around them. Yet still the little group of English believers lived and worked on in the wilderness, singing and shaking and practicing their peculiar beliefs apart from the world.

And then, in nearby Lebanon, in June 1779, a curious thing happened. There was a religious revival. It was similar to the revivals the Shakers had known in Lancashire. It was similar to those that had sprung up before in young America in the 1730s and '40s. Face to face with what seemed like Armageddon—the gathering of the English and American armies—anxious men and women who wanted no part of the conflict turned to God. They flocked to New Lebanon, not far from Niskayuna, to be saved at the great meetings held in a big barn. The nightly scenes at the barn were very like the scenes at a Shaker meeting: screamings and faintings and prophetic outpourings.

However, no one at the camp meetings had a solution to America's ills. Many of the people who had come to hear the word of God on the country's problems left disillusioned. They felt they had heard nothing new.

Then, by accident, two of the disillusioned New Lebanon Seekers came upon the band of holy strangers who lived sinlessly in a small log cabin. At least that was how the two described the Shakers. The description was enough to send many others to the Shaker encampment.

The original two who had found the Shakers were Talmadge Bishop and Reuben Wight. What had happened to them when they stumbled into Niskayuna was this: They were greeted with the news that their waiting time was over. Christ, they were told, was not *going* to come, He had in fact returned already in the person of Mother Ann. And then came the solutions. The Shakers by now had a real program of salvation to offer, not just the vague words and prophetic utterances of the New Lebanon revival. They offered a regular series of actions and activities to be performed. Celibacy, communal ownership of goods, and the equality of the sexes were the backbone of the sect. In addition, they preached total pacifism, confession of sins, and the belief that resurrection depended upon each individual and his or her acceptance of the life of the spirit. And most of all, they believed in singing, dancing, and plenty of hard work.

Bishop and Wight did not know what to make of the Shakers, but they were impressed by the sincerity and ardor of the group. So the two men hurried back to New

Lebanon to tell the Reverend Joseph Meacham of their discovery. Meacham, who had been a mover behind the revival and one of its most ardent seekers after a new truth, lost no time in finding out more about the Believers.

He sent his assistant, Calvin Harlow, to talk with them. Harlow came back a changed man. He returned claiming that Mother Ann was, indeed, the long-awaited Second Coming.

Meacham could trust no more messengers—he went himself. Accompanied by his two closest ministers, he set off into the Niskayuna wilderness.

What a strange and striking meeting it must have been. On the one side of the small log cabin stood the English Shakers with the gray-clad, fiery-eyed Mother Ann at their head. On the other side stood the tall, grave American Meacham with his two friends by his side. They spoke for hours, verbally sparring, quoting Scripture at one another, citing church history and Bible history. And all the while, Meacham's hazel eyes bore into Mother Ann's blue ones, searching, seeking answers.

At last, according to Shaker tradition, Meacham asked the final challenge: "Are *you* perfect? Do *you* live without sin?"

It was Whittaker who took up the challenge. Yes, the Shakers lived completely without sin.

And, Mother Ann added, they lived without sin because they forsook "the marriage of the flesh."

Meacham was convinced—so convinced he left his own church, where he was the minister, and became a Shaker.

Mother Ann called him her "first born son" and prophesied he would gather in the rest of the church after she died.

It was the beginning of the Shaker "millennium" that lasted two hundred years. And for at least fifty years, the people did, indeed, come to the Shakers "like doves."

The conversion of Meacham was a turning point. With him came a good number of his own congregation of New Light Baptists from New Lebanon. He also attracted many of the seekers who had looked for truth in the revival barn. They found it instead in the Shakers' swampy clearing.

These are some of the truths they found:

> *The marriage of the flesh is a covenant*
> *with death, and an agreement with hell.*
> *If you want to marry, you may marry*
> *the Lord Jesus Christ.*
>
> —MOTHER ANN

> *If you give your minds to labour upon*
> *the things of the world, they will*
> *become corrupted.*
>
> —JAMES WHITTAKER

Over and above all the Shakers emphasized the necessity of hard work. This was not a comfortable religion they were offering. In Mother Ann's words—based on a folk saying common to European peasants—they must work as though they had a thousand years to live and as if they knew they must die tomorrow.

Practicality was a cornerstone of the faith. Mother Ann had seen poverty grind down her neighbors and friends and she had a great fear of it. Firm foundations and sturdy houses and plenty of good plain food were therefore important to her. However, Mother Ann had also seen the church spend great sums of money on frills and decoration while some of its followers starved. *Her* faith would have none of it. The Believers would not be paupers, but they would never be allowed to dwell upon the things of this world, the *unimportant* things: fancy dress, ornate furnishings, lush foods, even the keeping of such useless pets as dogs and cats as long as there were poor, down-trodden people.

Mother Ann's conversations with her companions and with her community were sprinkled with folksy wisdom. Her most important maxim was "Put your hands to work, put your hearts to God."

And so they did. But while the Shakers put their hands to the work of building their community and their hearts to the worship of the God of their devising, they ignored the world at large. In their ignorance, they ran afoul of their neighbors.

It happened in the early spring and summer of 1780, when many folk were coming to Niskayuna and staying on for days or even weeks. The problem of feeding such multitudes was a difficult one. Though often the seekers themselves brought along food, the Shakers had to search out new sources of supplies.

The country was then hard at war, fighting for its independence from England. This rounding up of food was seen by some of the local New York patriots as a plot to aid the British. When they caught three Shaker farmers of New Lebanon driving in their own sheep, the patriots dragged the three to court. The farmers were accused of trying to spirit the food off to the British army. After all, it was well known the Shakers were against the American cause. First, they were newly arrived English men and women, and second they were outspoken against the war. (The fact that the Shakers were against *both* sides in the war was ignored.) The farmers were thrown in jail.

Within days, six more Shakers were in jail, including William Lee, John Partington, James Whittaker, and Mother Ann.

Mother Ann was kept the longest. She was not let out until December, almost five months later. It is said that she continually pressed her face to the window bars of her cell and preached to the people who gathered outside.

The Shakers had been set free when the authorities realized that, far from being traitors, the Shakers were a hardworking religious sect with little or no influence. But the authorities realized that a little late. By the time the Shakers had been set free, they were no longer a little-known group. The trial and subsequent jailing had made them famous. They were national figures.

As soon as the Shakers were free of the jails, they began the hard work of being traveling missionaries. For two years they traveled through wildernesses and thirty-six towns. They touched many lives. They were also touched again by trouble.

Mobs set upon Mother Ann not once but many times. She was stoned, beaten, struck with sticks and fists. Once, in Petersham, New Hampshire, she was dragged by the feet out of the house where she was staying and thrown onto a sleigh like "the dead carcase of a beast." The men, who ripped her clothes and beat her, said they just wanted to see if she was a woman or a man. They could not believe that a woman had the strength of purpose, mind, and body to lead a religious sect.

The Shaker men fared scarcely any better. They were dragged from houses, beaten with clubs and whips until their backs bled. Their heads and ribs were broken. Even the elderly Shaker men were set upon by bloodthirsty mobs.

Even though none of the Shakers was killed outright by the mobs, the incredible harsh treatment shortened all of their lives.

In fact, Mother Ann's brother, the personable William Lee, died at age forty-four, ten months after the missionaries returned to Niskayuna in September 1783. It was said that he died from the aftereffects of a fractured skull.

Mother Ann herself never fully recovered from the difficult trip. Slowly her strength ebbed away. The final blow was her brother William's death. As she weakened, her visions became stronger. Often she had dreams about her impending death.

Such visions and dreams frightened her followers, who counted heavily on her guidance. She soothed them, saying: "Do not worry. You will see peaceable times, and none of the wicked will make you afraid."

She settled back into the rhythm of the Niskayuna community. The year that followed her missionary trip was simply a year of a slow slide into death. Before she died, several of her visions were recorded by the Shakers. In 1784 she dreamed of Brother William in a golden chariot taking her home. At the same time, she saw that "the next opening of the gospel will be in the Southwest." And she also saw that Meacham would preside over a Shaker church that would be gathered into "a united body."

A few days before her death Hocknell had a vision of his own. He said he saw Mother Ann's soul going to heaven in a chariot drawn by four white horses.

Mother Ann died on September 8, 1784 at the age of forty-eight. Hundreds came to her funeral—Believers and unbelievers alike. She was buried at Niskayuna in a humble grave.

But the movement Ann Lee had begun did not die. From the exhausting trips she made through Massachusetts and Connecticut were left the outlines of Shaker colonies to come. Small groups of Believers were seeded in Hancock, Tyringham, Harvard, and Shirley, Massachusetts, and in Enfield, Connecticut. They would grow, indeed, into a mighty tree.

Mother's love I want to feel,
Father William's power,
The innocence of Father James
O heaven on me shower.
—ROUND DANCE, NEW GLOUCESTER, 1856

Two Fathers and a Mother:
1784—1821

6 THE Shaker movement did not die with Mother Ann, but it suffered a severe shock. Many of her followers had simply not believed that Ann Lee *could* die. They believed she would live until the Judgment Day. And when she died an ordinary human death, some of them lost their faith and left. One of these was John Partington, who had come all the way from England with John Hocknell.

But the core remained. To lead them was the thirty-three-year-old James Whittaker.

Father James was the perfect leader for this period in Shaker history. He was a fiery speaker, a fiercely loyal believer, and one of the original English Shakers. Also, Father James was a passionate defender of the chaste life. He felt that the young Shaker movement was in danger of temptation as long as the brethren and sisters were in close touch with the real world. So Father James prepared the

Shakers to take the step that would remove them from the hostile, sinful world.

It was Mother Ann who gave the Shakers their ideas and ideals.

It was Father James who gave them their community.

Only three days after he became the new leader, Father James began a year-long series of visits to the scattered groups of Shakers. He traveled from Maine to Massachusetts himself. He sent his most trusted lieutenants to organize the Connecticut Believers. The idea was to centralize the groups, bring them together and take them away from the outside world.

So full of vigor and hope were the Shakers under Father James's fierce and purposeful hand, they raised the first meeting house in New Lebanon in 1785, during that first year of his travels. It was a stark, gambrel-roofed building that was to symbolize the Shaker ideal: plainness and strength.

With the completion of that first meeting house came Father James's call to order: "Gospel Order." This was the discipline that the communities were to follow. Later, it would be the most obvious, outward sign of Shaker life. Father James's Gospel Order read, in part, "Ye shall come in and go out of this house with reverence and godly fear. All men shall come in and go out at the West doors and gates; and all women at the East doors and gates. Men and women shall not intermix in this house or yard, nor sit together; neither shall there be any whispering or talking or laughing or unnecessary going out and in, in times of public worship."

Father James was strict with his companions, but he was stricter with himself. He spent his strength so prodigally that he wore himself out. Within three years of assuming the leadership, he was dead. He was just thirty-six.

Father Joseph Meacham was left in charge of the home church of New Lebanon and Mother Lucy Wright was set in charge of "the female line."

Except for Mother Ann, these three—Father James, Father Joseph and Mother Lucy—were the three most important leaders the Shakers had. Each had a singular place in the history of the sect:

Mother Ann gave the Shakers their ideas and ideals.

Father James gave them their community.

Father Joseph made the scattered groups a United Church.

Mother Lucy sowed the Shaker seed in the West.

Succession in a church group is not always easy. How do people judge who is worthy to follow in the footsteps of God? Do they vote? Do they choose lots? For the Shakers, whose members wait upon heavenly guidance before proceeding, the wait *could* be long indeed—or it could take a peculiar turn. However, the transition from Father James to Father Joseph was relatively smooth. For one thing, Father Joseph had already been a leader in many activities, both with the Shakers and before he joined them. Bright, well-spoken, organized, and energetic, he had been called by Mother Ann herself "the wisest man that has been born of a woman in six hundred years." He was also extremely pious and devoted. When Father James had died in July, the other Believers noticed that Father Joseph, standing by the graveside, had trembled like a tree in a storm, shaking "from head to foot."

It was no real surprise, then, when at the first prayer meeting following the burial, one of the assembled Shakers rose and declared in ringing tones that Father Joseph was meant to be the new leader. He had been, after all, called by Mother Ann her "first Bishop." There was no dissension.

One of Father Joseph's first acts was to raise the strong-willed Mother Lucy Wright to "lead the female line." This act set a pattern for the Shakers, one that was far in advance of its time. For here, in the midst of a century in which women were counted as property, the Shakers established a dual order of government in which men and women were considered copartners. Except for the Quakers, where men and women had equal say, no other church group ritualized sexual equality. And in fact, in most religious groups, women were definitely downgraded.

Catholics and Protestants had no women priests. In Judaism there were no women rabbis. But in the Shaker communities women as well as men had the visions that moved the group; women as well as men ruled in both religious and secular matters. Most important, women as well as men were the supreme leaders of the Shakers, from Mother Ann to the present day.

By September 1787, three years after Mother Ann's death, thirteen years since the Shakers' arrival in America, the Believers were ready to take the final step that would separate them inalterably from the world. No longer would they live in scattered family groups throughout New England. Rather, guided by Father Joseph, they would gather in large communities, hold all property in common, and live and work together.

The word went out. Father Joseph and Mother Lucy, the parents of the new order, called their children home— home to New Lebanon. The meeting house had been built and was waiting. Members in New Lebanon had donated houses and land. Come home, come home, the call went out.

And the Shakers came home.

They came from all over New England, filling every building in the area. They moved into huts, into cabins, into barns, and into sheds. From September through December, they traveled, sometimes through the heavy New England snows. They came home to New Lebanon, where their parents in the faith waited.

And on Christmas Day, 1787, the Shakers sat down in the meeting house for their first communal meal.

Men sat with men, women with women, the children by themselves. It marked the end of family life as any of them had known it. It signaled the official rising up of the United Society of Believers in Christ's Second Appearing.

What had begun as a spiritual adventure in England was on that Christmas Day brought to fruition. The United Society, a series of independent village communes, was begun.

The headquarters for the Society remained in New Lebanon where the sole meeting house stood. Members there, gathered in "Society Order," began working out the rules that would govern their lives together.

What a time it must have been for the Shakers. So many men and women, singly and in whole families, had come to live the Shaker life that the Believers literally hoped to save the entire world. And so they talked of, built for, and farmed for the thousands upon thousands they believed it was their destiny to convert, house, and feed.

The New Hampshire Shaker, Moses Johnson, who had framed that first meeting house in New Lebanon, was in such demand because of the Shaker hope that he was nine years traveling from community to community overseeing the building of more meeting houses. Those plain, strong, many-doored, spireless meeting houses still stand.

Ten years after Mother Ann's death, the roll call of the Shaker communities sounded like an American poem:

Harvard, Hancock,
Tyringham, Shirley,
Canterbury, Alfred,
Enfield, too.
New Lebanon, New Gloucester,
Niskayuna.

To the Shaker men and women it was still not enough. There was still more work to be done. "Work as though you would live for a thousand years, work as though you would die tomorrow." Mother Ann had said it. The Shakers lived it.

Father Joseph's chosen work was to consolidate the Shaker gains. He wanted to be sure that the Shakers would not lose what they already had. He began a written contract, a covenant, that had to be signed by each new convert. According to this covenant, a convert who decided to become a Shaker for life must legally sign over his or her entire property to the Shakers.

Father Joseph also brought more and more people under Shaker roofs, and his organizational ability provided that each new member would be sheltered well, fed well, and made a part of the Shaker whole.

But the work killed Father Joseph as it had his predecessors. In 1796, scarcely nine years after he began his work, Father Joseph was dead. He too had died of exhaustion.

Mother Lucy continued alone.

By now, all was peaceful and calm within the well-run communes. For several years the singing Shaker meetings moved along without interruption. Men and women worked at their separate but more or less equal tasks. Children were brought into the community either as part of the converting families or as orphans adopted by the Shakers. No new babies were conceived and born there.

However, in 1804 the outside world suddenly forced its way into the Shaker consciousness. A new religious revival had begun on the American frontier. In Ohio, Tennessee, and Kentucky men and women and children were coming together and being afflicted by "the jerks." Reports of these phenomena came to Mother Lucy's ears and she was troubled. Could these be yet-to-be-born Shakers? She remembered the prophecy that Mother Ann had made some thirty years before: The next opening of the gospel would be in the Southwest. Was this what Mother Ann meant?

Mother Lucy wrestled with the problem by herself. The reports of new sects whose members were seized with strange paroxysms, whose members fell into deep trances, whose members twisted and jerked and sang and barked like dogs kept coming in. And then the answer came to Mother Lucy in a vision. The Shakers must farm the fallow ground of the frontier.

New Year's Day, 1805. With Mother Lucy's blessing singing them on, three men and one horse departed from the New Lebanon community. They would travel over a thousand wilderness miles before they reached their goal.

The trio of missionaries pressed through New York, Philadelphia, Baltimore, Washington, then crossed over the wild Appalachian Mountains. They did not stay more than a single night in any one place until, by accident, they reached a small log cabin in Turtle Creek, Ohio. It was two months and twenty-two days since they had left home. They stayed with a frontiersman that night. He was Malcolm Worley. Worley confessed his sins and became the first Shaker convert in the West.

Worley introduced the three Shakers to his pastor, the educated Presbyterian minister Richard McNemar. The three won McNemar over, too. He joined the United Church and brought along his entire congregation, much as the Rev. Joseph Meacham had done twenty-six years before.

The missionaries wrote back joyfully to New Lebanon: "Here was a people waiting for us."

If anything, the three Shaker missionaries underestimated the numbers waiting. They found they needed more money to keep the new communities going. So Brother Issachar, one of the three, had to walk all the way back to New Lebanon by himself for the needed help.

And so, added to the American poem, were the following:

> *North Union, South Union,*
> *Union Village,*
> *Pleasant Hill, Whittaker,*
> *Watervliet*

Only one Western community failed in those first years. In Busro, Indiana, it was not a crisis of faith that killed the commune; rather, the community fell victim to bouts of malaria, Indian raids, and frequent occupation by brutal Indian-chasing soldiers. The members reluctantly left Busro and joined other Shaker settlements in more peaceful surroundings.

Slowly, the sturdy little settlements grew. They grew

despite some persecutions and despite the fact that no children were ever born within their gates. They grew and
prospered in both the East and the West until, by the Civil
War, there were eighteen societies divided into fifty-eight
units called, surprisingly, "families." They grew until the
original eight English Shakers had become six thousand
American Shakers. And all were working hard and sharing
everything in their lives because, as one writer put it, "they
were certain God's kingdom had come and they were living
in it, unmarried and unsullied as angels."

Awake my soul arise and shake,
No time to ever ponder,
Keep awake, keep awake
Lest ye be rent asunder.

—FROM SOUTH UNION

The Peak and the Decline:
1806—Today

7 THE Shakers grew and grew. They fought battles both within and without, but still they continued growing.

One problem was disease. In the farthest flung frontier communities, sickness was always rampant. Malaria had helped close the young colony at Busro, and the other groups had their own attacks of whooping cough, measles, and mumps.

Another problem was the continuing religious prejudice and the wild rumors that followed wherever the Shakers moved. Common among the rumors was that each member considered himself or herself to be a Christ and that each boasted of eternal life. It is simple to see how such rumors began. The Shakers believed that God is within every person who confesses sin and becomes a Shaker, and said so. How could death frighten a people who believed they were already living in the heaven that had been created on earth?

More destructive than the rumors by people who did not know any better were the shrill, angry pamphlets by apostate Shakers. An apostate is a person who once believed in a religion and subsequently left it. The apostate Shakers wrote wildly distorted things about the Believers. They claimed the leadership were drunkards who held wild revels and debauches while keeping the rest of the Shakers in celibate slavery. They claimed that the Shakers danced naked and cursed God in secret mountain hideaways or captured orphan children for cruel practices too horrid to mention. One of the bitterest of the ex-Shakers was Mary Dyer who had been a member of the Enfield, New Hampshire, community. Her *Portraiture of Shakerism*, written in 1822, called Mother Ann a hypocrite, a prostitute, a sadist, and a drunk. She was scarcely kinder to the others.

Such tales grew bigger and sillier and crueler as they traveled from person to person. The result of such rumor-mongering was always trouble for the Shakers. No matter how wild the story, there were people ready to believe the worst. Shaker houses were burned, fences torn down, horses mutilated, cattle let loose in grainfields.

The worst of the mob scenes occurred in Union Village on August 27, 1810, when five hundred armed men backed by a thousand angry followers charged into the peaceful community. They had heard that the Shakers held orphan children captive and had come to set them free. But there were no children enslaved, of course, and the mob left, its ugly mood only slightly abated. Similar incidents in 1813, 1817, 1819, and 1824 occurred in other Shaker communities.

Despite the sicknesses, the rumors, the mobs, the Shakers continued to grow, until the time came early in Mother Lucy's reign to set down accurately, in print, exactly what it meant to be a Shaker. There had been papers and pamphlets before; the contracts signed by Shakers were examples of pledges and commitments. But the Shakers felt a need for an official defense against the anti-Shaker mobs and the anti-Shaker movements. The ministers who were going out trying to win converts in the West carried with them Joseph Meacham's *Statement*, but it was not adequate for their needs. The ministers, and many others in the Shaker movement, had only the vaguest notion of Shaker theology and Shaker history. They knew only that being a Shaker worked.

And so, Elder Benjamin Youngs, one of the three missionaries who went out West, wrote what was the first authoritative work on the Shaker church. It was called "The Testimony of Christ's Second Appearing." He wrote it in a bare attic room in one of the new houses built by Shakers in the West.

He sent the manuscript to Mother Lucy in July 1806. She approved it, saying, "I am sensible that what you have written is the Gift of God."

The book was printed and widely distributed two years later. It is a document that explains the basis for Shakerism and exalts the life of self-denial. It says, for example, "But this I say, brethren, the time is short: it remaineth, that both they that have wives be as though they had none; and they that weep, as though they wept not; and they that rejoice, as though they rejoiced not; and they that buy, as though they possessed not; and they that use this world, as not abusing it . . ." The language is the language of the Bible.

As the Society grew, it opened its doors to people of diverse races and religions. No other American religion except the Quakers had dared do such a thing. Blacks as well as whites, Catholics as well as Jews, even members of the various Indian tribes were invited to join. What made this the more startling was that these different people were invited not *just* to worship with the Shakers, but to live side by side with them, working and sharing equally in all things.

Some of the blacks were slaves who joined with their masters in the early days of the movement in the West. The question of slavery was an important one to these communities before the Civil War. But it was only in 1819 that the Shaker slaves were generally emancipated; by 1830 the last Shaker slave was freed.

Though at one time there was a segregated community

of forty ex-slaves, most of the Shakers lived in *integrated* harmony. This arrangement came directly from Ann Lee, for her message was without doubt antislavery. One of her visions, recorded in her *Testimonies*, told of seeing the blacks saved from their low estate and riding in the sky with crowns on their heads.

The number of Shakers grew until ten years before the Civil War. At that time there were six thousand members in eighteen communities with fifty-eight church "families." The Society owned $5,000,000 worth of property. But after the 1850s, though many of the diseases were conquered and the main prejudices and mob violence had been overcome, gradually but perceptibly the Shaker movement began to decline.

The Shakers felt that a decline was inevitable. They said there was a natural cycle of growth and decay. Mother Ann herself had more than once said that the movement would eventually decline until there would not be enough Shakers left to bury their dead. She had grasped, intuitively, the fragile nature of the perfection she and her companions were seeking. She had understood how in the planting is the harvest, how after harvest comes decay.

The factors that led to the Shakers' decay, to their slow, steady decline, are important to understand. A society that is created as a sanctuary from the temptations and hardships of the world often attracts people for other than religious reasons. Certainly there were many misfits within the Shaker ranks, men and women who could not deal with the world at large, people who could not make a living, who needed to be with a large, protecting "family." And there was another phenomenon peculiar to Believers. They let into the communities what they called "winter Shakers," people who joined for food and shelter over the harsh New England winters. (In the Israeli kibbutzim today there is a similar phenomenon: young travelers who stay and live off the community for a few weeks or months before disappearing back into the hitchhiking life.) For these kinds of "Shakers," the religious belief was secondary to the way of life. They did not necessarily believe in the doctrines, in the confession of sins, or that Mother Ann was the Second Coming of God. But they believed in the hot meals and in giving work in exchange for shelter. The very presence of these semi-believers helped water down the religious commitment of the community. Their presence might make uncertain souls, or impressionable young people, question the beliefs on which the Shakers based their lives. Yet the winter Shakers were never turned away.

Another problem was that the goal of communities was self-sufficiency. Yet as America became more and more industrialized, the effect upon communities that relied on handwork as one of their sources of income was disastrous. Who would buy handmade goods when machine-made products were cheaper? Even the Shakers themselves discovered they could purchase machine-made cloth for much less than the cost of making it themselves. It was in such small savings that their end began, for as they relied more on the outside, industrialized world, their uniqueness began to die.

Then, too, the Industrial Revolution brought with it

a move from the countryside to the cities, and even the children brought up by the Shakers succumbed to the lure of city life.

Also, the Shakers had overspent their money on land. They were land-poor; that is, they owned more land by the 1850s than they could properly cultivate. Yet still they bought small farms, wood lots, even mills in far distant states. To try to make that land pay for itself, the Shakers began to hire outside labor or to rent out portions of the farmable acreage. It was clearly against their own beliefs of separation, against the Shaker tradition of dealing with the outside world as little as possible. But it was a necessary compromise if they were going to be able to pay the taxes on their land. The Shakers, who prided themselves on being free of lusts, had succumbed to one of the oldest sins of the world—the lust for land. It was another factor in their downfall.

In addition to the land that lost them money, the Shakers had another money problem. Around the time of the Civil War, a number of the communities lost money because of speculation in small businesses or because of bad debts. At North Union, for example, the community lost $12,000 when unscrupulous lawyers and land agents robbed them. Union Village lost even more, $40,000 in all. Those were enormous sums at that time. As one community suffered, the others gathered around to help. And so the money problem of one Shaker group became the money problem of all.

A continuing problem was the matter of recruiting new

members. No new members could be born within the society because of the ban on marriage and sexual relations. (An occasional baby was born of newly accepted members who moved into the Shaker community after the wife was pregnant.) There was no larger noncelibate Shaker community from which to draw celibate members. Within the Catholic Church, for example, only the monks, priests, and nuns are celibate, but they come from the ever-growing population of noncelibate Catholics. The Shakers, though, waited for new members to hear the call and join them just as they waited to hear directly from God. Fewer and fewer outsiders heard that difficult call. Fewer and fewer new members were found.

Finally, perhaps the most important reason for their decline, was what was missing. After Mother Lucy's death in 1821, there was no one strong spiritual guide for the Shakers. There was no one strong zealot to rekindle the spiritual light. Instead, the clamorers, the reformers, the men and women who were willing to compromise with the outside world came to power. It watered down the Shaker experience and dampened the fire of the faith. Though the latter-day Shakers still believed in the Shaker truths, they believed less spectacularly, less frenetically, less loudly. They were less willing to suffer and die for their beliefs. They were comfortable and wanted to remain that way. By the end of the nineteenth century, the Shakers stopped their religious dancing. Organ music took the place of the vast choirs of Believers. The shaking, trembling visions of glory were no more.

The most noteworthy of the new Shaker leaders was Elder Frederick Evans of New Lebanon. A radical Englishman who had come to America in 1820, Evans was a vigorous pamphleteer. He had been associated in England with his brother in publishing works that advocated such forward-thinking stands as equal rights for women, freedom of public lands, and the abolition of debtors' prisons. Evans continued his outspoken career even after he joined the Shakers, though his views were colored slightly by his new religion. He suggested that both the presidency and governorships be dual offices. He advocated that the national and state senates be open only to women, the lower houses only to men. He further stated that the leadership of the country should be in the hands of a class of "intellectual celibates," men and women who would be married only to the state. These leaders were to be brought up and trained in "spiritual granaries" such as the Shaker communities.

Evans was a strange, strong-willed, dogmatic man full of personal charisma. Even though a number of his ideas alienated many people—including many Shakers—he was considered one of the official spokesmen for the Shakers. He was their leading intellectual, and carried on correspondence with the outside world, with the Russian author Tolstoy and the American social reformer Henry George. In the Civil War, it was Evans who petitioned President Lincoln for draft exemptions for the pacifist Shakers—and won.

Through the influence of Evans, some of the strictness

and conservative tendencies within the Shaker movement began to crumble. Evans preached that the Shakers needed to understand the outside world, not merely to be removed from it. Newspapers and magazines and books on such worldly subjects as history and travel began to find their way into the Shakers' houses. Evans' argument was this: Saints were as deserving of the good things of the world as sinners.

Slowly, but inevitably, one Shaker community after another dissolved. Six villages closed forever between 1875 and 1900. To aid the still living, thriving villages, the moribund or dead properties were sold. The Shakers moved in together, consolidated.

The decline looked something like this:

    1850: six thousand members

    1900: one thousand seven hundred members

    1960: last male member, Delmar Wilson, died.

The history of the birth, growth and decline of the Shakers is not too different from that of any other small religious sect. There is a definite pattern. First comes the total emotional and physical commitment of the founders who are willing to give up all for their beliefs. Then comes a need for strict organization. But the organization itself begins to take the place of the beliefs, of the simplicity on which most small sects are based. And there are few converts won over to a staid, established sect. It is the radicalness, the fire, of the new that is inviting. If there is no way to create members from within, the sect will slowly decline.

It happened that way with the Shakers.

In 1957, when there were fewer than fifty Shakers left, a decision was made to close the doors to any new members. The decision was made by the Canterbury ministry. The remaining sisters at Sabbathday Lake made a vigorous but doomed dissent.

With a spiritual bang, the Shaker doors slammed shut.

And when we find ourselves
In the place just right.
'Twill be in the valley
Of love and delight.
　　　—SONG "SIMPLE GIFTS," 1848

The Valley of Love and Delight

8 THE Shaker communities were not haphazard homes.
Every one and every thing had a place. Theology became rule, custom became law. If it had not been so de-
fined, the communities would not have lasted as long as
they did.

For example, the Shakers believed that men and women
must have no sexual contact with one another. It was basic
to their religious belief. Without abstinence, they felt, men
and women could not be as the angels. But to enforce this
belief, to make it workable in their everyday lives, the
Shakers set down laws to help themselves. Men and women
lived in separate houses or, if circumstances forced them
to live in one house, on separate floors. They came and
went through separate doors, walked on separate staircases.
They ate at separate tables, held separate jobs within the
communities. Even the children were kept separated, boys

with boys, girls with girls. And all this was spelled out in their rules. If, despite all the separateness, a man and woman fell in love and wanted to marry, the Shakers had provisions for that, too. At the Tyringham community, for example, the two lovers went to the Elders and were then put on a six-month probation. After this thinking time, if the two still wanted to be married, the Shakers let them go into the world with a blessing, a sack of flour, a horse, and a hundred dollars. It was not a small dowry. Many young people of the outside world married with much less of a settlement. But this kind of marrying did not often happen in the Shaker communities.

Or take another example: the Shakers believed that the "things of the world" had a corrupting influence. They felt that once men and women and children began to desire "things," such greed never stopped. It got in the way of worship. Therefore it was Shaker practice to be as plain as possible, to make clothing, houses, furniture, tools as simple and as use-oriented as could be. Anything frivolous or vain or useless was forbidden. Custom became law. Shaker dress was the epitome of plainness. The women wore pleated white gowns covered by blue and white aprons. Large neckerchiefs chastely covered the bosom, white muslin caps covered the hair. The men wore blue coats, blue and white pantaloons, black waistcoats. They dressed simply and the same.

Shaker furniture was also simple, with concession to neither decoration nor padding. All this was at a time when

the outside world was making elaborate furniture and dress. Often clothing and furniture were beautiful and uncomfortable. The Shakers, though, believed that the form of an object must follow, as closely as possible, its function. In other words, an object—furniture, or tool, or a dress—must be simple and directly made. Nothing must stand in the way of the "use" of that object. At the same time, everything the Shakers made reflected their virtues: honesty, humility, temperance and simplicity. Nowhere is this more apparent than in Shaker furniture. The beauty, for the Shakers, was not in excess decoration, but rather in the direct usefulness of each piece of furniture.

To contemporary outsiders, though, the Shaker emphasis on plainness did not seem beautiful—it often seemed

just plain dull or grim. Charles Dickens, the nineteenth century novelist, wrote nastily after a visit to a Shaker community: "We walked into a grim room, where several grim hats were hanging on grim pegs, and the time was grimly told by a grim clock which uttered every tick with a kind of struggle, as if it broke the grim silence reluctantly and under protest. Ranged against the wall were six or eight stiff high-backed chairs and they partook so strongly of the general grimness, that one would have much rather have sat on the floor than incurred the smallest obligation to any of them."

All the rules and laws were to help the Shakers in their desire to withdraw from the world. They wished to become independent of the world, self-sufficient. To this end, the

Shakers isolated any newcomers to their ranks, allowing only the oldest and most pious Believers to have any contact with them.

An incoming Shaker had to go through a ritual of divestment. He or she had to wind up all business affairs, pay off any outstanding debts, break off ties with relatives and friends. Only then could the newcomer enter a Shaker community, bringing along whatever was left: livestock, wagons, bed, bedclothes, seed, grains, pots, and pans.

For the newcomer, that was only the beginning. First the new arrival was received into a novitiate order, a beginning order. It was called the "gathering family." Here newcomers were allowed to keep the property they had brought in and to stay within their own family unit. But if they decided to take the next step, entering into the "Junior order," they had to dedicate their property to the Shaker community. (If they decided to leave the Shakers, their property, at this point, was still recoverable.)

When the new Shakers wished to become members of the highest order, they had to sign over everything they owned without reservation. It was Father Joseph Meacham who had instituted this final, legal covenantal step in the 1790s. Once the final step was taken, the individual member owned nothing, the Society owned all. Even if a member backslid, decided to leave the order, he or she could take nothing away from the community legally.

What did the members of the order do? What did they

work at? The simplest answer is *everything*. The adult Shakers were masters of many different trades. They had to be, since they were trying to develop a self-sufficient community. The brothers were stonemasons, accountants, beekeepers, herbalists, carpenters, distillers, tailors. The sisters were nurses, housekeepers, laundresses, seam-stresses, jam-makers, cooks. Interestingly, even though they believed in the equality of the sexes, men did "men's work" and women did the lighter housekeeping chores. Only occasionally did a man do weaving or a woman do the heavier outdoor chores. It was simply a question of strength. (It wasn't until the twentieth century, when there were too few men to carry on the traditional work of the brethren, that the sisters took over many of the men's jobs.) No one was overworked, but no one was ever idle. As newspaperman Horace Greeley wrote of them in the nine-teenth century, theirs was "constant but never excessive toil." And it was everchanging toil, too. No Shaker, being required to do so many different tasks, ever felt a monotony in the work. And always the task was done neatly, in orderly fashion, with great care. Even—or especially—the housekeeping was done in this fashion for, as the Shakers reminded one another, "good spirits will not live where there is dirt." The Shakers became known for their precise workmanship. It was the way they honored Mother Ann's maxim, "Hands to work, hearts to God."

They honored her revolutionary doctrine of equality but separateness of the sexes in their church hierarchy, too.

The head of the church was divided into a ministry of equal numbers of men and women, usually two of each. In every community there were several "families"—not families of husbands and wives, but families that consisted of thirty to ninety people. Each of these extended families was ruled by two elders, a male and a female. Their duties, according to the Shaker rules, were "to teach, exhort, and lead the family in spiritual concerns." Next in line were deacons and deaconesses, and after them male and female trustees. Each family had a number or a name, such as Center family, South family, Hill family.

It was a giant pyramid, with the New Lebanon ministry at the top, led by a Mother and a Father. But always, women were responsible for the women, men for the men.

The children brought in with their mothers and fathers and the adopted orphans had their place, also. They were educated and cared for by loving adults in their extended families and were expected to follow the Shaker way. So they were taught in Shaker schools, apprenticed in the necessary and appropriate trades, and instructed always to follow their "gift" or spiritual promptings.

The children had no toys from the outside world. These were frivolous and useless. But as one young Shaker girl at Niskayuna wrote: "We . . . were just as contented with our corn-cob dolls, clamshell plates, acorn-top cups, and chicken coops for baby houses."

Yet for all the attention and loving care given the Shaker

children by an army of mother-aunt or father-uncle sub-
stitutes, few of the children raised by the Shakers stayed
with them. Only one or two in ten chose to remain in the
Valley of Love and Delight.

And so each day was ordered for the Shakers, for the
men and women and children, too. A typical day might go
like this:

At four o'clock on a summer morning, a bell or "shell"
awoke the sleeping community, rung by the Shaker in
charge that particular day or week. (Winter hours were
somewhat later.) Then they all prayed silently for a few
moments. At a signal, each member of the "retiring rooms"
(for they shared large bedrooms) stripped his or her own
cot of sheets and blankets and pillows and laid the bedclothes on two chairs at the bedfoot. This all took fifteen
minutes, performed as fluidly as a dance.

The brethren went immediately to their chores around
the house and farm. When they had left their rooms, the
sisters came into the men's rooms and set them in order.
They remade the beds, changed the linen, hung up chairs
and clothing on the high pegboards that lined every Shaker
room. The floors were kept as free as possible of clutter to
make sweeping and cleaning easier. The only thing the
women did not touch were the chamber pots which had
been emptied already by the men. Everything was done
with the precise movements of a close-order march.

By six or six-thirty it was time for breakfast, for the

morning chores were done. The fires had all been started—
by the men—food prepared, cows milked, animals fed. But
it was not yet time to sit and eat. First there came the
"broad grace," fifteen minutes in which men and women,
in separate rooms, waited in silence for the breakfast bell.
And when it rang, there was no hurried scuffling and
scrambling for places. Even the children were mannerly.
In two columns, men in one and women in the other, led by
the elders and eldresses in the order in which they were
to be seated, the Shakers filed into the dining hall.

When they entered the room, they marched solemnly to
the proper table and waited behind the chair or bench
where they were to sit. At another signal they knelt for
prayer. Then they sat down for a silent meal. They ate
sitting upright, following the elders' or eldresses' lead. And
when each was done, according to the ninth rule of the
table, each "cleaned plate, knife & fork—lay(ed) bones
in a snug heap by the side of plate—scrape(d) up crumbs
—cross(ed) knife & fork on the plate with the edge towards
the chair," and waited for the final prayer. Everything was
eaten, nothing was wasted. It was called "Shakering your
plate."

Then and only then did the main chores of the day
begin. Those Shakers with a particular "gift" worked at
that particular trade, the others took turns with the farm
and household chores.

Children, too, had their days set for them. Especially
after 1808, when education on a regular basis was begun,
the children had chores and classes. Spelling, reading,

writing, and good manners were taught. Later such things as geography, grammar, algebra, astronomy, and agricultural chemistry were gradually introduced. Their recreation and games tended to be useful: gymnastic exercises to keep the young bodies in trim, cultivating flower gardens, nutting and berrying parties, and the like. The children—boys with boys, girls with girls—ate and slept in their own order. But the girls at fourteen and the boys at sixteen left the children's groups to take their places as responsible Shaker adults.

For all, adults and children, the work day was broken by the noon dinner and the six o'clock supper, performed in the same ritual manner as breakfast.

After the evening chores were finished, around seven-thirty, the Shakers went to their rooms. There they spent half an hour in silent prayer, sitting erect with hands folded. This was known as "retiring time," though it was not a time of sleep. This quiet time, after a full meal and a hard day's work, often lulled a tired Shaker to sleep. If one dozed off, he or she had to stand up and bow or shake four times before sitting down again.

At a bell signal, the Shakers left their rooms, formed their separate columns, marched two abreast to the main meeting room, bowed as they entered, and came inside to worship. A typical weekday meeting took about an hour, for by nine in the winter and ten in the summer, after kneeling by their beds in silent prayer, the Shakers finally went to sleep.

When we assemble here to worship God,
To sing his praises & to hear his word
We will walk softly.
    —"WALK SOFTLY," EARLY ANTHEM

Walking Softly:
Shaker Ceremonies

9 THE ordered work day of the Shakers had its quiet
   times for prayers. The day began and ended with
silent worship. But the wild, shaking meetings of the first
Believers were not gone entirely. Instead they had under-
gone a change, a neatening; they had been given a place in
the orderly structure.

Once the Shakers had settled into a daily pattern, once
their lives became rigidly prescribed, their ceremonies became rituals. The frenetic shakings gave way to special
dances; the shrieking and speaking in tongues became
songs. The strange gestures and uncontrolled leapings
were given names and functions. And only occasionally,
during set times in the rituals, were the Shakers allowed
to shake.

However, the isolation of communities led to the de-
velopment of exotic rituals. Even a simple event can be

the starting point for a new rite. For example, a few days before Mother Ann's death at Niskayuna in 1784, a young sister named Hannah Goodrich was sweeping the piazza floor with care. Mother Ann saw her and came outside.

"Sweep clean," said Mother Ann.

Young Hannah looked up and replied, "I will, Mother."

But the sick woman repeated distractedly, "Ah, sweep clean, I say."

The girl answered again, "I will, Mother."

Yet a third time Mother Ann said, "But I say, sweep clean."

In another house, in another kind of community, with another kind of woman the sick person might have been ignored or gently put to bed with a sleeping potion. But not in a Shaker community where every utterance of Mother Ann's was given a mystical interpretation. She was, after all, believed to be God. Young Hannah, who would go on to be the first Mother of the Canterbury-Enfield bishopric, understood the strange conversation differently. She "perceived that Mother had reference to the floor of the heart" and reported the incident to the elders. After Mother Ann's death, a sweeping ritual was established in all the Shaker communities. A special day was set aside for a general cleaning of all the houses and buildings.

The sweeping day was not simply a cleaning day, however. Hannah's perception of the sweeping as having to do with an inner cleansing was important. While one group of Believers was doing the physical work of sweeping, another group of singers and elders marched through the community carrying "spiritual brooms." They sang and chanted and swept with invisible tools, singing special songs such as:

Sweep, sweep and cleanse your floor,
Mother's standing at the door.

While the sweeping ritual was a special ceremony, "retiring time" was an everyday occurrence. That was the name given to the half hour of meditation that preceded weekday evening worship and the entire Sabbathday worship as well.

The worship meeting had its own rules and regulations. If the worship meeting was held in the meeting house, the Shakers marched to and from the hall in "church order," files of two with the elders in the lead, sisters following the brethren. The men marched in through the door on the right, the women on the left. Not a word could be spoken as they filed in to take their places, places according to position in the society, age, sex.

Inside the meeting house, the Shakers sat on long benches, women on one side of the hall, men on the other, in parallel rows. Hands quietly folded on laps, the Shakers waited in silence for a signal.

Either a preacher or the presiding elder gave the signal, a bell or a nod of the head. Then the Shakers arose in a body, removed the benches to the walls, clearing a large space in the hall.

There was singing then, some doctrinal hymn about the meaning of being a Shaker. Perhaps they sang:

When we assemble here to worship God
To sing his praises & to hear his word
We will walk softly.

Then there might be a discourse or talk by one of the elders. As the Shaker movement grew older and bigger, there were special marches and dance songs, elaborate as a ballet. They were performed with strict steps and movements. But occasionally things would get out of hand and an orderly meeting would turn into what the Shakers called "quick meetings" or "Shaker highs." And only then would the trembling and shaking and crying out resemble the early Shaker meetings.

In the period from 1842 to 1845, the Sabbath meetings began to be regularly disrupted by Shaker highs. The sisters screamed and trembled and the young boys called on spirits that were bringing them "gifts." The men leaped and whirled and called out in tongues while young girls made strange "spirit drawings" they claimed came from visiting angels. When these things began to happen with increasing frequency, the Shaker meetings were closed to the world's visitors. It wasn't until 1845 that most of the spirits, according to the Shakers, "took their departure" and the meetings were again open to the world. But what is left from that period of Shaker highs is an incredible legacy of primitive drawings, pages decorated with birds and flowers and angels that rank among the most beautiful and interesting contributions to America's folk art.

If every day was a worship day and the Sabbath a time of many meetings, there were a number of special feast days as well. In 1842, a ritualistic mountain meeting was begun.

Each Shaker community chose a hill or mountain top as a site for what eventually became twice-yearly observances. The men cleared and leveled a half acre, inside of which was enclosed a small hexagonal plot of ground with a low fence. One side of the fence was marked by a marble tablet called the "fountain." It was not a place of real but of spiritual water.

The mountain sites were given special names, such as Mount of Olives, Chosen Square, Mount Assurance, Holy Hill.

The evening before the May and September feast days, each member of a family assembled in dim candlelight in the meeting room and knelt before the elders and eldresses. As each Shaker approached to kneel, the elders and eldresses reached into invisible chests and pulled out clothes that no one could see. These "heavenly garments" were passed out solemnly to every Shaker, and as solemnly put on—over their real clothes. Then each Believer bowed his thanks four times to the elders and eldresses and went off to bed.

The next morning, dressed in their spiritual garments—

carefully put on over their real clothes—the Shakers met at the church and marched two abreast up the hill.

On the hill, it is said they worshiped with song and dance "in which everyone acted independently." No one knows for sure. The ceremonies were secret and no one from the outside world was ever allowed to take part.

Those ceremonies are ended now; and the sacred stones, the "fountains" of spiritual water, have been buried or otherwise hidden from the world's eyes. Only one of the living sisters today knows where the stones are, and she has vowed to take that secret with her to the grave.

We'll take the choicest of their songs
Which to the Church of God belongs.
　　—HYMN XI, MILLENNIAL PRAISES,
　　HANCOCK, MASS.

The Gift of Song

10 FROM the beginning singing was a very important
part of the Shaker ecstatic worship, but the first
songs were without form. They were simply a trembling,
caroling, crooning, murmuring way of expressing what an
individual was feeling. In a life that was restrained,
bounded by "thou shalt nots" so rigid as to deny the most
basic human needs, such outbursts of song were one way
in which the Shaker spirit could find freedom of expression.
It was a necessary outlet.

But gradually the droning fragments from the psalms,
the babblings of "ho, ho, ho," the crooning "love, Mother's
love," and the shouted "hallelujahs" gave way to patterned songs. By the time the Shakers had been in America
fifty years, they had developed a large body of music
peculiar to their sect. The songs became part of a distinct
folk culture. For this, if for nothing else, the Shaker place
in history would be assured.

The first formless, wordless songs were very individual, even to the point of hurting a listener's ear. One United States congressman who was present at a Shaker ceremony reported later that the Shaker women were "howling sundry strange tunes." However, as often, visitors could recognize bits and fragments of old songs changed, corrupted almost beyond understanding. The tune might be a fragment of an old English melody or an Irish jig tune, in the first years of Shakerdom. Such a borrowing is understandable. None of the early Shakers was a trained musician. Few of them could even read. Of course they would incorporate into their singing snatches of melody with which they had been familiar in England. Such singing, humming, borrowing, had a childlike innocence, just as the songs created later would have.

When the New Light Baptists came into the Shaker fold in 1779, they brought with them some of the rousing Protestant hymns they had so loved. Later, the Ohio and Kentucky converts did the same.

As these new songs began to drift into the Shaker communities along with the new converts, the elders became worried. The tunes were universal, the words definitely Protestant. So Shaker words were put to the borrowed tunes. As one of the Shaker songs later recorded:

> *We'll take the choicest of their songs*
> *Which to the Church of God belongs*
> *And recompence them for their wrongs*
> *In singing their destruction.*

The fears of contamination led to a movement within the church to complete a body of Shaker songs. A kind of fierce song competition began.

Once a song was composed or created, the maker sang it for his or her family. Then the songs were sung again and again in weekday singing meetings. The singing meeting was begun just for this purpose and replaced a few of the worship meetings in the evening after retiring time. A song learned by one family would be quickly taught to another family. From community to community the Shaker songs traveled. Singing became part of the Shakers' everyday life.

Plain, somber songs were learned under the leadership of the dour Father Joseph, songs which were properly sung, according to his directive, "deep in the throat or breast." These gave way during Mother Lucy's ministry to "merry tunes." During her rule, in fact, a tune close to "Yankee Doodle" could be heard—with proper Shaker words, of course.

All this time, the Shakers were learning each and every song by rote. They memorized words and tunes. The problem was that no one knew how to read or write music. It was considered a frivolous pastime. But once the floodgates of melody were opened, it became necessary for the community's sake to note down the many songs "sent by God."

In 1807, therefore, musical notation was introduced into the Shaker villages. It was not an easy decision. Many of the older Shakers were against bringing this diversion from the outside world into their closed ranks.

Abram Whitney, a member of the Shirley society, had been a music teacher before he joined the Shakers. He single-handedly persuaded the Shaker hierarchy of the need for learning music. Once convinced, the Shakers kept Whitney busy traveling between Massachusetts and Connecticut teaching music theory to the communities of Believers.

By 1823, the Shakers now under the leadership of Seth Y. Wells, taught music in their schools—not just any music, though. Shaker music. The best singers were put in special classes, and music became an integral part of the growing Shaker society. But the songs were never sung

in harmony. That was considered too frivolous for the Shakers.

Between 1814 and 1834 there were an incredible number of hymns, anthems, elegies, welcome songs, dialogue, and history songs composed by those who were musically gifted. The songs were sung by all the Believers.

Suddenly, in 1837, the gift of writing descended upon all the Shakers. Men and women, boys and girls began writing songs. They claimed to hear these songs from the lips of angels or from the beaks of birds, from Mother Ann Lee dead some fifty years, or from Jesus Christ himself. So many new songs and tunes were turned out, the Shaker leaders had to make special provision for this gift from heaven. Many of the songs were beautifully inscribed light blue paper and bound in calf's hide. Only a few them were actually sung. They were simply kept in lection of "manifestation songs."

The "gift songs," as they were also later called when fourteen-year-old Ann Maria Goff of the Sou at Watervliet (Niskayuna) suddenly went into whirling trance with some of her companions. round they went, minute after minute. No them, for it was assumed they were God-inspir

Just as suddenly as they had begun, the Exhausted, they went to bed.

That night, Ann Maria and two of her f suddenly. They felt they could look dow bodies still asleep on the beds. When

their bodies, the other two girls were silent, but Ann Maria began to sing in a strange, high-pitched voice that did not sound at all like her:

"Where the pretty angels dwell, Heaven!
Where the pretty angels dwell forever."

Ann Maria was only the first of the children to claim she traveled to a spirit land and returned with a breath of song on her lips. Others quickly followed her lead. The children, encouraged by the adults and applauded by their friends, talked incessantly of places where they heard beautiful singing.

Of course this kind of thing was contagious. Before long, the adults, too, heard the spirit singing. Some sang in nonsense babbling they called foreign tongues. Others said they were bringing back songs in "negro dialect" or in Hottentot, Chinese, or Indian tongues. These were not the actual languages. Actually they were rather poor attempts at reproducing dialects or languages by an individual who had no real knowledge of the tongue.

One of the "Indian songs" went like this:

Me Indian come
Me come me stay
Me tanke de white man
He show me de way.

A song in an unknown tongue, begins:

Se-le-i as-ka-na va,
Ves-e-ven-ve-ne vi.

The gift of song did not wait upon a quiet moment when a pen was handy. Like any creative inspiration, the gift descended anywhere, anytime. Shaker journals noted that songs came to such divergent groups as those "on the mountain top blackberrying," "cutting apples," and "to the brethren splitting wood." The people did not have to wait for the word. It found them wherever they were.

And when the word came to them, it came in mysterious ways. The Shakers claimed to have learned the words and tunes from scrolls carried by doves or from the mouths of generals Washington and Lafayette, from golden chains swung by Muhammed or found during a trip to the moon. There seemed no end to the visionary experiences.

The songs created by the Shakers were unique. They sang of Shaker experiences, they celebrated Shaker visions, they put Shaker theology into rhyme. And surprisingly, they were fine folk songs, too. The structure—uses of repetition, the accompanying movements—were reminiscent of the playparty or game songs from the Appalachian Mountains.

It is not surprising that many of the songs survived, even past the influence of the Shakers. And one in particular, "Simple Gifts," has made its way into the more traditional churches of America, into school and camp repertories, and into American classical music as well.

'Tis the gift to be simple, 'tis the gift to be free,
'Tis the gift to come down where we ought to be,
And when we find ourselves in the place just right,
'Twill be in the valley of love and delight.

When true simplicity is gain'd,
To bow and to bend we shan't be asham'd.
To turn, turn will be our delight
Till by turning, turning we come round right.

When true simplicity is gain'd,
To bow and to bend we will not be asham'd.
—FROM "SIMPLE GIFTS," 1848

To Bow and To Bend:
Shaker Dances

11 J U S T as the Shaker songs grew from wordless, tune-less hums, so intricate and precise dances grew from the impassioned, formless miming done in worship.

"Miming" means a soundless acting out. That is pre-cisely what the earliest Shakers were doing, acting out their emotional, spiritual commitment during meetings: forty or fifty men and women springing up as if flying to heaven; men and women trembling as if struck by the fever of God; men and women making strange posing mo-tions with their arms, which the Shakers called "signs."

The Shakers called these miming exercises "laboring," for they believed they were working hard as they mimed, working to throw off the lusts of the flesh. And it *was* ex-hausting work, especially after a long day of physical labor in the fields or house.

Laboring had a purpose in Shaker terminology. It helped them to crucify their pride in self, to debase and simplify the body; it helped them prove that their bodies were nothing—their souls everything. But it was something more, something the Shakers never admitted to, perhaps never even understood. The frenetic dancing and posturing, even more than the singing, was a release from tension and from the restricted, separate, unworldly life they led.

Years later Shaker theologians tried to rationalize and give Scriptural reasons for their dances. In the 1820s and 1830s, Shaker scholars reminded themselves that there were many references in the Old Testament to dancing: Jephthah's daughter danced, the daughters of Shiloh danced, even King David danced before the Ark in the Bible.

Such Scriptural reassurances helped the Shaker belief that dancing served a divine function, that it was an exercise that joined body and spirit. Not all dancing, of course, was so divine. The outside world used dancing as an excuse for touching. But the Shakers danced in their worship meetings, and never did man touch woman or woman touch man.

As time passed and the Shakers were gathered into communities, that early impulsive dancing changed. Such individual miming and posturing was then given a new name: "promiscuous" and "quick" or dancing in the "back" manner.

In the period 1785–86, when the New Lebanon meeting house was built and Father Joseph began to impose an order on the communal life and worship, the dances underwent a radical change too. Father Joseph devised a special forward-and-backward square order dance in 1788. It was slow and solemn, just as he was. Father Joseph revealed that he had seen that very dance in a vision of angels moving before the heavenly throne. Since he was not a dancing man himself, he had practiced the steps alone in his room over and over before venturing to show them to the other Believers.

The Square Order Shuffle, as it was called, went like this: three steps backward, three steps forward, then a double step (tip-tap), then back three steps, tip-tap. The brethren were to set off on the left, the sisters on the right. Whether Brother Joseph knew it or not, this was a slow variation of a jolly Scottish country dance known as the Gay Gordons. But Father Joseph saw the dance as a solemn shuffle, and solemnly the Shakers danced it.

They danced the slow beat until 1796 when Father Joseph died. His death so shook the communities that for two years they did no dancing at all, just gathered in solemn, "weighty" meetings.

When two years of mourning had passed, the Shakers took up their simple solemn shuffle again. By this time, however, spirited Mother Lucy was firmly in charge. Her manner and mode were totally different from Father Joseph's. Where he was calm, deliberate, conscientious, she was outgoing, volatile, gay. Mother Lucy also had a vision of angels dancing before the heavenly throne. But her angels were not marching solemnly in a square order shuffle. Instead they were skipping buoyantly before God, filled with joy.

This new vision directly affected the Shaker way of worship. The square order shuffle, while still danced, was done in a lighter, faster, gayer way. The old "promiscuous" dancing came back. And while the older, staider Shakers were not particularly pleased with the change, the children and young people (who were brought in after 1805 in the frontier revivals, the second "gathering of the church") were delighted. Indeed, it seemed as if Mother Lucy had reinstated Mother Ann's original cry, "Be joyful brethren and sisters! Be joyful! Joy away! Rejoice in the God of your salvation."

Mother Lucy brought many new dances to the Shakers. Not only were the dances quick and lively, but many new kinds of dances were introduced. Under Mother Lucy, special gestures in the exercise songs were begun in 1815, marches in 1817. Soon after Mother Lucy's death in 1822,

ring dances started up in the Shaker communities. Instead of mourning danceless, the Shakers continued Mother Lucy's manner. It was as if her gay, irrepressible spirit were still leading them on.

The new marches had such names as "Sermon March," "Little Children's March," and even "The Strawberry March," which was chanted by the sisters as they strode with sprightly steps to and from the strawberry fields. The names were not fanciful. Rather they were descriptions, and strongly reminiscent of the country and square dances from which many of them sprang. "Winding March," "Lively Ring," "Moving Square," "Mother's Square," "Mother's Star," "Cross and Diamond," "Elder Benjamin's Cross," "Endless Chain," and "Wheel Dance" were but a few.

Between 1822 and 1825, many new dances were tried out. A visitor to the communities might witness practice at any time. The brothers and sisters moved in ranks, double file, through the yards and the orchards, even going up and down the highway, marching and singing.

The Shakers practiced continuously. By the 1830s, the Shaker dances were so well rehearsed that the brothers and sisters could have gone on tour as a professional folk dance company, had they so chosen. Such rehearsal was necessary. By this time, the dances had such intricate and complicated patterns that only by constant practice could the Shakers hope to remember the many steps. In fact, a Mr. Henry Tudor wrote, after visiting New Lebanon on July 14, 1831, "[It was] one of the most extraordinary scenes . . .

that I have ever witnessed in any of the four quarters of the globe."

There were other witnesses as well. By the 1830s, special benches were set around the barnlike meeting rooms for visitors. The dances were popular Sunday afternoon entertainment. While three or four hundred Shakers joined the intricate patterned dances, singing and dancing for their God, the "world's people" watched from the sidelines. Curious outsiders would often drive in their carriages for miles to watch the Shakers circle and march and dance on the broad unvarnished floors.

The dances they watched—though pretty, formalized, and complicated country dances—were concrete expressions of Shaker theology. For example, four concentric circles of dancers symbolized the four dispensations or spiritual cycles of Shaker belief; the marches were meant as metaphors for the soul's trip toward heaven.

Yet as measured and solemn or sprightly and precise as all these dances were, there were often times when they would suddenly shift and change as the service became emotionally charged. Suddenly, individuals would break into the whirling, shouting, leaping, stomping orgy of God-glorification: a Shaker high.

Some of the visitors called them "penguins in procession" and laughed even as they watched. But others saw in the Shaker dancing a "sacred beauty" and in their posturing "a very noble symbolism." Whatever the visitors' thoughts, the Shakers did not care but continued to mime and shake and dance to their God in their own way.

I love I love the gifts of God,
I love to be partaker
And I will labor day & night
To be an honest Shaker.

— NORTH UNION, OHIO
SQUARE ORDER SHUFFLE SONG

Hands to Work

12 THERE is a Shaker story that tells how a sister watched one hot morning as two brethren sweated and strained over a two-man saw. She saw not the men but the problem: two working at backbreaking, sweaty labor and producing very little for their effort.

The sister's mind went to work on the problem, seeking a simple, functional solution. Suddenly it came to her, a gift from God. That sister invented the world's first circular saw, a saw that wasted not a bit of motion.

The Shakers built such a saw to her specifications at once and set it going at Watervliet (Niskayuna). Using the saw, one man and one boy could do as much work in one day as thirty men had done before.

It is not an uncommon story in Shaker history. In fact, the Shakers were famous for their inventions, inventions that improved efficiency and thereby increased the time the Believers had available for study and for

· 95 ·

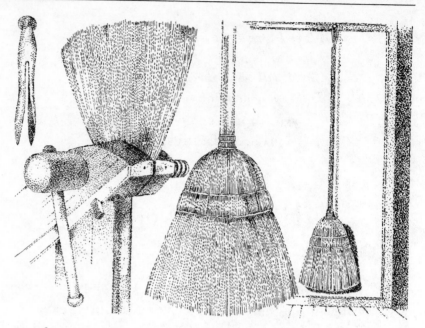

worship. Among their other inventions are the flat broom, the wooden clothes pin, the screw propeller, the washing machine, the threshing machine, the double-chambered wood stove, water repellent cloth, and oval nesting boxes— all timesaving and laborsaving devices.

The Shakers also contributed enormously to the growing science of agriculture with their horse rakes and harrows, ideas on breeding livestock, and experiments with silage.

They were the first in the country to produce metric measuring devices under a license from the United States Government in the 1870s.

Of all these inventions, the Shakers patented only four: the chimney cap, the washing machine, a metal button that was affixed to the base of a tilting chair, and a folding

pocket stereoscope for viewing pictures in three dimensions. Basically, the Shakers did not believe in accepting royalties for patents. The ideas, the inventions were gifts from God. Let the world's people profit from such, the Shakers felt. They, themselves, would not.

However, unlike other separatist groups, the Shakers did not spurn the gifts. The Amish in Pennsylvania, for example, refused to accept the progress of the Industrial Revolution. To this day they will not use electricity or zippers. Their houses and farms are run on candle and horse power. Their clothes close with buttons. But the Shakers never refused those inventions that bought them time for their God.

While they would not accept money from their inventions, they did profit from other commercial ventures. The

Shakers were America's first commercial seedsmen. Beginning their business in 1790, the Shakers shipped grains and seeds all over the world. In the last century, it was not uncommon to see the Shaker brethren in their broad-brimmed hats on the road in one-horse peddler's wagons selling Shaker seeds and furniture and home remedies to a growing market.

The world was fast becoming aware of two things: Shaker handiwork and Shaker honesty.

The standards of workmanship the Shakers set were high. The products they made more than one hundred years ago are still usable. Shaker baskets and boxes and tables and chairs, Shaker buckets and hay forks, grain measures and rakes can still be found, elegant in their simple lines, and strong enough for work. The Shakers built for eternity, not for the marketplace. They built for their own use or to carry the Shaker name forward. So the buyers always knew that Shaker work could be trusted, and that Shaker guarantees could be believed.

Always, of course, simplicity was emphasized. In Elder Frederick Evans' words, they felt they "had no right to waste money upon what you would call beauty . . . while there are people living in misery." All Shaker products had order, harmony, utility—but no ornamentation. The Shakers emphasized the making, not the selling.

The Shakers were not rich, though their communities were well-tended and large. Rural, in an ever-increasingly

urban world, the Shakers made handicrafts and furniture of a passing age. Still, there was a demand for what they made and grew, and they struggled with their diminishing numbers to fill the demand.

The seed business was an ongoing success. Not only were the garden seeds popular, but medicinal herbs and dried sweet corn were popular as well. The crafts that continued selling included the Shaker brooms, chairs, nesting boxes, baskets, chair mats, small brushes, blankets, shirts, capes, and rugs.

As the product line expanded, the Shaker women began to demand a more active role in the selling of their work. And as the number of men in the communities grew fewer the women were able to take over their jobs. The sisters began to make the regular tours of the mountain and seaside resorts, the country fairs and marts, dressed in their Shaker outfits, bonnets firmly tied in place.

Where the early Shakers had had to suffer the brutish handling of the mobs, these selling Shakers had to endure nothing more than some giggling and stares. For the most part the Shakers now had the approval of the commonfolk. Their hard work and honest labor and the beauty of their products spoke for them in the world's marketplace.

Today, besides a high-priced trade in Shaker antiques, reproductions of Shaker furniture, boxes, and cloaks sell extremely well. Antique ladderback Shaker chairs with the original seats and the ball casters go from $150 to $250 at auctions. The Shaker rockers are even higher, on up to

$450. The nesting boxes bring from $20 apiece on up to
$150. Several national magazines advertise kits for build-
ing "your own Shaker furniture." A roomful of dollhouse
furniture modeled on Shaker lines was recently advertised
at $200. And there are modern craftspeople who make
their living copying the simple, functional Shaker line. In
fact, in New York a few years ago, a store called Shaker
House opened with the specific intention of selling clothes
and furniture "in the Shaker tradition."

Mother Ann often repeated "Hands to work, hearts to
God" and the Shakers always tried to follow her words.
They prayed with their whole hearts, and their hands shaped
objects that carried their theology even into the homes of
people who could never accept their God.

O come Mother's little children,
Wake up wake up,
O come Mother's little children,
Wake up, keep the fire burning.

   —UNION VILLAGE SONG

Open to Visitors

Sabbathday Lake, July 19, 1975

13 ROUTE 26 runs through the heart of the last living Shaker community. It is a fast, noisy road that brings Canadian travelers down to the Maine beaches.

Yet Sabbathday Lake is peaceful despite it. After all, what can one road mean to a community that has existed in the same place for almost two hundred years?

The road brings hundreds of tourists who visit this Shaker community and buy Shaker-made products: postcards with Sabbathday Lake buildings pictured; notepaper with samples of the spirit drawings; records with the high, sweet voices of the sisters singing Shaker songs; books about the Shakers in America; and always the famous Shaker herbs and teas. From here the word goes forth, the word spreads. If it were not for that noisy Route 26, life in the fast-paced, wheeled world might totally pass the Shakers by.

The Shakers have never refused progress. Rather they have used it to fill their own spiritual needs, used it on their own spiritual terms. As one of the sisters at Sabbathday Lake has written, "It is . . . not the world which the Believers must shun, but only those things which may come between the Believers and God."

But it is progress that has dealt the Shakers their death blow, at least so all the textbooks say. However, this small handful at Sabbathday Lake refuses to let go of the Shaker way. Sabbathday Lake, in these Believers' words, is the "stone of stumbling" to those who proclaim the Shakers dead.

"Nay," replied Brother Ted Johnson firmly when asked if this was the end of the great experiment. Brother Ted is the director of the Shaker Museum at Sabbathday Lake. He felt that the death of the Shakers has been grossly ex- aggerated. Interest in the Shakers is still running high. Books continue to be written about them. Other religious groups on retreat stay at this community.

Legally, however, the end of the Shakers may be near. The few old Shaker women who live at Canterbury, on the advice of worldly lawyers closed off covenantal entrance to the Shakers in 1957. Though a person still can come and stay his or her entire life within a Shaker community, there is no way legally to become a Shaker, to sign the covenant that Father Joseph made a part of the Shaker way. When the last of the covenantal Shaker women dies, the Society's large trust fund and properties will go to a foundation for charitable purposes and for the preservation of the archives, cemeteries, and Shaker museums.

Yet Seekers still come here. Not like doves, perhaps, in the great flocks that Mother Ann had prophesied so long ago, but by ones and twos.

Dr. Ted Johnson is a good example. A highly educated man, he found out about the Shakers through scholarly means. He has been living and working with the Shakers since 1960. But he is not covenantally a Shaker. That is, he has not been allowed to sign the last covenant that would put him in the third order of Shakers. Still he lives at Sabbathday Lake and works there as Brother Ted, giving all he earns to the community.

Brother David has been there four years. Brother Steven, an eighteen-year-old high school graduate, has been there well over a year.

These men have joined hand and heart with the redoubtable women who are the remnants of a once-flourishing society. Sister Frances, with her brusque, engaging openness; Sister Mildred Barker, a tiny bird of a woman with a remarkable sense of humor who has been a Shaker since she was seven; and the five others still alive and working at Sabbathday Lake.

Where once the Shakers pointed with pride to the fact that they worked shorter hours than the world's people because there were so many Believers working in so organ-

ized a way, now each of the remaining Shakers puts in a twelve-to-seventeen-hour day in order to make this last piece of Shakerdom a going concern.

But so much is gone.

Gone is that strict division between men and women. Where once they met only in such work as needed both or at the worship meetings, now there is constant conferring, crossing. Sister Frances and Brother Ted talking in the upstairs hall of the Main Dwelling House about window shades; Brother Daniel clearing the luncheon table and bringing dishes into the sisters' well-organized kitchen; Sister Mildred and Brother Ted bidding me a farewell together by the side of my car.

Gone is the strict dress code that made Shakers immediately recognized anywhere. Though I knew the code had been officially set aside in 1900, it was with a shock that I realized the pleasant-faced woman in Bermuda shorts walking down the hill toward my car was a Shaker. It was Sister Frances on her way to the herbary. At lunch she was more traditionally attired in a longish dress with a yoke across the bosom. Brother David wore a work shirt and jeans. Brother Ted was in short sleeves because of the summer heat. Young Brother Steven was shirtless, in cutoffs, as he worked in the garden.

Gone is the strict injunction against useless animals. Two gentle dogs roam the grounds. Argos, an old German shepherd, is Brother Ted's particular pet. Sister Frances and Sister Mildred seem to be the special caretakers of Melissa Rue, a mongrel.

· 107 ·

Gone are the silent dinners when there were so many Shakers at Sabbathday Lake they had to eat in shifts. Instead the Believers here eat in a chattering hubbub, and often the conversation crosses between the men's table and the women's table.

Gone are the massive shaking, dancing meetings. Instead, the small group—occasionally augmented by friends —gathers weekdays in the dining room and Sundays at the Main Meeting Hall. There they hold slightly structured worship services with the singing of two Shaker songs, a reading from Scripture, and a homily. Silence usually follows. Though the Believers still occasionally dance a few steps and gesture with their hands on some songs, the shaking, trembling ecstasy of the old meetings is gone.

To modern eyes, the Shakers seem remarkably lacking in those prejudices that most of America carried through its early days—racism, sexism, and a propensity toward violence. The Shakers anticipated many twentieth-century ideas and moralities. They made equality *for all people* a working part of their religion, their lives. Even the emphasis on simplicity and lack of ornament seems right to us today. The Shakers built communes in America when others were building individual fortunes, spoke rapturously to God with their hearts while others were communicating unreasonably with their heads, and refused to parade their wealth so long as there existed others less fortunate than they.

Yet so much of the Shakers is past history. So much is gone.

What is left besides the antiques, the houses and barns, the museums of Shaker crafts, the herbs and nesting boxes? The joy in life, the joy in work, the joy in community are still at Sabbathday Lake as they were in the original Shaker communities. And *these* are the not so simple gifts that Mother Ann has bequeathed all her children.

· 109 ·

BOOKS FOR FURTHER READING

All the books about the Shakers are for adults or older boys and girls. But if you want to read more about this "peculiar" people, some of the following books are especially recommended.

Andrews, Edward Deming, *The Gift to Be Simple*, New York: Dover, 1962. (Andrews is the most famous of the Shaker scholars, and this study of Shaker songs and dances is the only book of its kind. Andrews and his wife made studying the Shakers their life's work.)

————, *The People Called Shakers*, New York: Dover, 1963. (This book is *the* classic study of Shakerism, though Brother Ted Johnson at Sabbathday Lake feels Andrews made many assumptions about Shakerism that were not true.)

Desroche, Henri, *The American Shakers: From Neo Christianity to Pre-socialism*, Amherst, Massachusetts: University of Massachusetts Press, 1971. (A difficult but fascinating study by an ex-monk.)

Faber, Doris, *The Perfect Life*, New York: Farrar, Straus and Giroux, 1974. (Interesting journalistic approach to the Shakers by a newspaperwoman. Written for older boys and girls, 12 and up.)

Johnson, Theodore, *Hands to Work and Hearts to God*, Brunswick, Maine; Bowdoin College Museum of Art, 1969. (Brother Ted as director of the Shaker Museum wrote the essay which accompanies this collection of fine photographs of Shaker furniture and design.)

Lassiter, William Lawrence, *Shaker Architecture*, New York: Bonanza Books, 1966. (Detailed plans and architectural drawings of Shaker houses and barns.)

Melcher, Marguerite Fellows, *The Shaker Adventure*, Cleveland: Case Western Reserve University, 1968. (A full and fascinating account of the Shakers from Toad Lane in England to the Shaker Legacy.)

Morse, Flo, *Yankee Communes*, New York: Harcourt Brace Jovanovich, 1971. (A flowing account of the different commune societies that existed in America's past with an idiosyncratic but moving look at the Shakers.)

Nordhoff, Charles, *The Communistic Societies of the United States*, New York: Schocken, 1965. (A reprint of an account by the *Mutiny on the Bounty* author who visited the Shakers in the turn of the century.)

Sears, Clara Endicott, *Gleanings from Old Shaker Journals*, Boston: Houghton Mifflin Co., 1916. (This book makes for fascinating reading because it comes from the mouths—and hearts—of the Shakers themselves.)

Williams, Stephen Guion, *Chosen Land, the Sabbathday Shakers*, Boston: David R. Godine, 1975. (Photographs by a young man who spent a month living at Sabbathday Lake. Warm and loving photographs of the last living Shaker community.)

INDEX

Alfred community, 46
Amish, 97
Anne (queen of England), 15
Anti-Shaker movements, 53

Barker, Sister Mildred, 105
Bible, 10, 34, 54, 90
Bishop, Talmadge, 33–34
Busro community, 49–50, 51

Camisards, 10–11, 22
Canterbury community, 5, 46, 62, 76
Catholic Church, 44, 54, 59
Civil War, 50, 54, 55, 58, 60
Converts, 31, 32–35, 36, 47, 49
    order of membership, 68–69
Cross and Diamond (dance), 93
Cunningham, Mr. and Mrs., 28–29, 30

Dances and dancing, 59, 78, 80, 89–94, 109

belief and theology of, 94
between 1822 and 1825, 93
forward-and-backward square order, 91
miming exercises, 89–90
rooms for visitors to watch, 94–95
Daniel, Brother, 107
David, Brother, 105
Declaration of Independence, 32
Dickens, Charles, 67
Dyer, Mary, 52

Elder Benjamin's Cross (dance), 93
Endless Chain (dance), 4, 93
Enfield community, 46, 52, 76
England, 7–24
Evans, Elder Frederick, 60–61, 98
Ezekiel, 12

Feast days, 79–80
Frances, Sister, 105, 107

ABOUT THE AUTHOR

JANE YOLEN is a prolific author of books for young people, including folk tales, fantasy, and biography. A graduate of Smith College, she is currently working on a doctoral degree in education and children's literature at the University of Massachusetts. She lives on a farm in Massachusetts with her husband and three children.